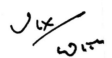

Black Box

Pete Langman

Published by Marvelhouse Words, 2014.

ISBN-13: 978-0-9575662-2-4

To life's survivors

black box

foreword   i
acknowledgements   iii

no regrets   1
airport and aerosol   7
the leper colony   15
nigel, prince of darkness   21
hardly a pumpkin   37
april fool   41
don't disturb mr. evans   47
christian soldiers   51
bandwagon   57
i talk to the wind   67
turning, point?   79
the old man and the sea   83
a short, dark season   89

foreword

A foreword is a dangerous place for a writer. It takes very little to move from a straightforward explanation of the whys and wherefores into an apologia. But I wish no more to engage in false modesty than in excessive self promotion. These stories represent those pieces written between the late 90s and the present day that I consider worth reading. Some more so than others. You, as reader, will not gain much by my explaining how this story was a dream, that story was an exercise, and so forth. With one exception: a short, dark season.

A short, dark season was written as an insert for a novel long since written and which sits exactly where it ought, in the bottom drawer. It is, in itself, rather special, in that most of the events described within it are matters of history rather than fiction. My grandfather was in Burma when the Japanese invaded, working as an oil man. He escaped relatively unscathed, unlike so many others. Perhaps touched by survivor's guilt, he set about collecting stories from other refugees of the time. I found these stories in his effects after his death in 1998. From these first-hand accounts, I built up the narrative that is a short, dark season. The events it describes are real, the people it describes are real, though I mixed up events and people not only to suit my narrative but to prevent the story being simply biographical. My sources were primarily the memoirs of my grandfather, Geoffrey Grindle, and two correspondents of his, Cherie Crowley and Bill Maclachlan. I have lost touch with the latter pair, but their stories are used with their full permission and approval.

Now little is left except to wish you happy reading.

acknowledgements

I have several people to thank with regards this book. My readers, especially Nadine Akkerman and Helen Masacz, my mother, for her input when I wrote a short, dark season (though she's also pretty cool), my grandfather, G.A.F. Grindle for being an obsessive compulsive hoarder of stories, and Ann Buckingham.

The magnificent cover was created by the really rather talented Helen Masacz, formatted by Rob Blackham, and I did everything else.

black box

no regrets

I felt your final, involuntary shudder as we drew together, and the surprise of penetration overtook you. That bitter, wet and bloody kiss that was to be our parting snapshot, the culmination of a series of incidents of disagreement, disruption and disharmony. I heard the air as it was forced from your body, the breath of life evicted as the knife cut, slicing its way through clothing and skin, finding its true home in the warm, sticky glow of the abdomen.

It feels strange. You hold the blade and gently excise the life of one you love. For today the blade is a token of love; the ultimate expression of my devotion. You become omniscient, omnipotent, omnipresent as your universe shrinks to the size of a small crescent-shaped opening. You focus on the wound, on the smooth yet granular blood which covers both of you, a pinprick of warmth which spreads slowly outwards and gently, heating the skin like a lover's tongue. This blood, the true elixir of life, takes on personality, its embarrassment at its sudden appearance soon turning into delight as it soaks through fabric, forming a sodden, bulging knot of fluid before it begins to drip, and soon it is running, cheerfully and mischievously, down your legs and towards the floor. At this point the wound is shared. There is no-one but you, joined in bloody union as you leak out, forming a thick, steaming pool at your feet. There are ripples forming around your shoes as you shuffle backwards and forwards, attempting to keep the balance between you, trying to stop your intertwined limbs from hitting the floor. A casual observer, catching sight of you through the kitchen window in an idle moment, bored of the myriad mundane tasks confronting the housebound, or walking idly by, would think you were dancing, and would probably breathe a sigh, remembering those times when they, too would dance in the kitchen for no reason. They would not see the pool on which you danced, they would perhaps mention it in passing to an acquaintance or partner. They'd never connect it with the story that will appear in the local rag.

It would be commonplace to state that time, at a time like this, stands still. Nothing could be further from the truth. From the moment we kissed, and the moment that the blade, held steady in my hand, entered the flesh, gently probing, pushing aside the life in its path, I could see it slip away. I could see it in your face, the horror within those cold, blue eyes, the pain wheeling into focus as it reached the seat of your consciousness, the despair as the truth followed, snapping at its heels. Time did not stop, it did no such thing. It didn't even have the good grace to slow down. Time sped up, accelerated for both of us, as our lives, in differing ways, leaked out onto the kitchen floor. They say that at the moment before you die, your life flashes before your eyes. Whether this is true or not I cannot say. All that we saw was each other. If you were truly my life, and I were truly yours, then maybe it does happen that way. You won't ask me now, even if you could.

You spoke, I think, though I can't clearly remember, it's all so long ago, so distant and hazy, that though barely a minute has passed since our embrace, the pain is already beginning to dull, the memory fade. As it will. And what use do I have for memories now? If you spoke, you spoke to yourself, not to me. I was merely within earshot, a coincidental audience. Sorry, were you awake?

2

Still, I see you standing there, above me, staring down at me with an expression that could only be a mixture of horror and pity, though neither is what I want from you. Neither is what I ever wanted from you. It was not meant to be like this. Not horror, not pity, but love. That's all I ask of you. But now all I can see is the wide, dull stain of livid crimson which is forming on you. It spreads like a cancer; slow, inexorable and malevolent. Strange how the harbinger of life is the same thing which denotes its removal. Blood exerts a strange pull, invites an almost morbid fascination. Many can't stand the sight of it. But for me, for us, context is everything. I notice how it appears different in hue through your white T-shirt and your black jeans. It brightens the light, signalling its appearance like a beacon, a flame of coughing life, that simply says; I am here. In the dark it grows thick and shadowy, attempting to melt into the background while making its purpose painfully apparent. It changes as it crawls from the light to the dark, the high to the low, from life to death as it seeks the lowest denominator it can. After all, its future lies in the earth, not the body. That was merely its temporary resting place. What are we, after all? Merely a place where all the molecules that make us are resting until they decide it is time to move on. Death is merely when our molecular structure becomes bored. Our atoms initiate inertia, and the change begins. It is all the same, of course, but to you, to me, to you, it changes. The longer it is active, the less time it has left.

And our time is almost up. You are holding the butt of the knife yourself now, gripping it tight in both hands at the height at which it entered. Waist height. The parallels are too obvious, even for me. The knife. You wrested it from my grasp. With the strength of desperation, I suppose, though I'll never know.

I'm also not sure whether your action was to remove it; and if so, why? whether it was to separate us; and if so, why? or whether it was to keep us together for those final moments. Our relationship, our long partnership, has ended with as final a mark of punctuation as can be imagined. And still I'm not sure. Indecisive to the end. Our life together. Over. No more parties, no more journeys, no more holidays, no more arguments, no future, no past, no present. No children. Our child. Our child, as yet unborn, sees its future. It sees its future as it turns its back and walks slowly away.

No regrets, no recriminations. No tears, no explanations. No guilt, no blame. That is what we promised each other when we first met, in those giddy days of love and lust and expectation. We would be forever honest with each other. Drunk on new love and old wine, we talked, laughed, argued, laughed, discussed, laughed, pontificated, laughed, made love and laughed. This was where we truly came together. Without honesty there could be no relationship. How long have we agreed on that now? How long is it? Do you remember? Do you remember the time that we first met? I do. Do you remember the weather? I do. Do you remember the way we laughed, the way we were? I do. I remember it all too well. It's a pity that you seem to have forgotten it all. Don't you think?

There was, as far as I could see, no greater honesty than in my action. As we made our final embrace, I took my leave of us. No regrets, no recriminations. No explanations, no guilt, no blame. Only the one, solitary, tear. I could see it even now, as your fingers relaxed their grip on the knife and it gently fell. I could hear it scrape its path slowly down your cheek as the knife hit the floor, rattling briefly at my feet before settling in the pool of its creation.

One single, solitary, tear. Was that all I was to you? That's honesty, I suppose. I could see (or, at least, I could imagine I could see) your life drain from you when I looked into your eyes as the knife entered. Could they truly register surprise at my method? Had you not realised that this was to happen, that this had to happen? I knew no other way. But what left your eyes was not your life. I was mistaken, I can see that now. What left your eyes was us. The concept of us. The concept of us as a partnership was what died in you. My action had ended not one life, but two. But it had not ended yet, not quite yet.

No regrets, no recriminations. No explanations, no guilt, no blame. One tear. But anger. Oh, there is anger. Anger as I see you, stained with the blood of our failed union, standing impassively over me as I lie, writhing on the floor, wet and sticky as the fluid drains ever more slowly from my body, and that which manages to escape fresh and warm coagulates ever more quickly. The pain, so long a stranger, has returned, and the cold realisation sets in just as the blood cools, no longer steaming, no longer the messenger of life. Now the information it carries is very different. The life which leaves is mine. Doubtless you could see it in my eyes, if only you cared to look, but you never did, did you? Each pulse, each beat of my still living heart is weaker now, but my anger is growing. Too late. I realise far too late what it is I've done. I realise far too late just how futile my action is.

Too late to change my mind. By depriving you of me, I looked to deprive you of life itself. Certainly, without you I would have none. And for months now I have been without you. What's made it unbearable is that you've always been there. Those eyes have always been there, staring back at me, empty, silent, accusing. Something missing. The light. That light which made my life worthwhile had gone. Given to another without so much as a by your leave. I don't know what it was that I did. You never cared to share it with me. All I know is that it couldn't carry on. Not like that.

I have, with my final act, not so much deprived you of your reason to live, as made it easy for you to carry on. That tear was not meant for me, nor even for you, but for that far distant us that died long ago. It was good, wasn't it?

No regrets, no recriminations. No tears, no explanations. No guilt, no blame. Too late for that now. Unconditional love. That's what you wanted. Or so you said. Do you still say that now?

airport and aerosol

Winston Davies was a worried man. The terminal of the airport building confronted him, taunted him. It had loomed out of nowhere, out of the fog of his confusion. It was not just his confusion which was causing the fog. The terminal was swathed in the real stuff, too. Thick, swirling fog the like of which Winston hadn't seen since the fifties. Even now he could remember cycling home from school in pea-soupers so thick he couldn't actually see more than five yards in front of himself. He relied on his excellent knowledge of the roads, the way he cycled home usually, counting the potholes, one-by-one, until all forty-three were passed. He knew exactly how many seconds, at his usual peddling speed of sixty revolutions per minute, it took to get from one to the next. He knew exactly how far to the left or right he had to steer to hit the edge of the next one, rather than running straight through the middle of it. His bicycle had solid tyres, so that could prove a little unsettling. Once he had been thrown into a state of confusion by the strange lack of the traditional pothole at the end of Grafton Street, just when he turned left into North End Road. It had been filled in, he found out later, but it had completely disorientated him. Just like he was disorientated now. Why? He cycled with his eyes shut as often as he could, the rest of the time holding them fixed firmly on the ground ahead of his front wheel, watching the tarmacadam whiz by underneath it, counting the lines and the cigarette butts he passed. Talking all the while to his bear, Edward no. 5, who he kept in the basket at the front of the bicycle. He relied on him, and his hearing, to tell him when the traffic was approaching. In those days there was far less traffic, he preferred that, and the cars, buses and lorries were far noisier. He occasionally cycled into a horse and dray, but only if they were still and there was a bus nearby, as this would drown out the noise of the stationary horse. All horses make a noise when they're still. He had learnt that early on. His father worked at the brewery. But the pothole was gone. Filled in. He wasn't sure whether to veer the thirty-four degrees left to try to hit the next one, one minute and twenty-two seconds down the road, informing him to take the short-cut through the path to the playing fields, or not. This confusion lead to him having to open his eyes and look up. Winston had never liked opening his eyes and looking up. He only did it when absolutely necessary. He never found what he saw when he looked up to his liking, even then. He had also relied on his prediction that in a pea-souper this thick, there would be no-one else on the road. Today this prediction had let him down.

Winston had to look up now, he was in trouble. He knew that he wouldn't like what he saw, but he would have to look up nonetheless. What he saw was the terminal building rising up both out of, and into, into the fog, like a ship looming out at him, too late to turn, too late to sound the foghorn. He started to panic again, before stopping in the middle of the pathway and trying to calm himself with deep, slow breaths, just like his mother had always taught him. Lie down, breathe deeply. Six breaths a minute. He could hardly lie down, but he could breathe. As he slowed down his rate of aspiration, the terminal building seemed to retreat back into its protective covering, as if it were hiding from him, but whether to launch another surprise attack, or because it had been warned off by this demonstration of his self-control, Winston couldn't tell.

Winston never could tell these things. Suddenly he was jostled from behind, a man and his trolley laden with cases rammed into him. As Winston apologised the man swore at him, rage bursting out into the clammy and chill night air. Winston was in trouble, he knew this, he didn't have much time, he also knew this, but he stayed to help the man put his cases back onto his trolley. In fact, he put them all back while the man continued to harangue him. All Winston could do was apologise. Apologise for being so inconsiderate as to stand on the pathway when this man, obviously far more important and in far greater need than he, needed to get by. Apologise for not realising that the man wasn't looking where he was going. Apologising for the blood that was now seeping out through his trousers where the trolley had broken his skin. Apologise for the fact that the force of the collision had knocked his glasses off, and one of the lenses had fallen out. Winston looked but couldn't find it, then, as the man pushed his re-stacked trolley away, re-loaded in such a way that the cases would no longer fall off at the slightest provocation, Winston heard the dull crunch as the man found his lens for him. He didn't apologise. Winston considered it.

The terminal loomed again, but only in one eye. In the left it had no more outline or form than a blizzard. Winston walked through the electric doors, reaching out to open them and almost overbalancing as he prepared for the push that never came. He stood silent and dumbfounded again as the fog, the cold and the wetness of the outside air gave way to bright, stabbing lights and a stuffy, overdry heat which hit him from above. He looked around him, his one good eye taking in the scene, searching for the one thing that he needed.

Winston was scared now, as well as in trouble. Outside, he had been alone, but he was used to that. He had been in trouble, but he was used to that too. Now he was surrounded by noise and bustle and what seemed like mania. Everyone moving and jabbering and rushing and shouting and squealing, without seeming to either get anywhere or communicate anything. Modern life encapsulated. A throng of people, ugly, smelly, all achieving nothing and doing it with the maximum of irritation and noise, maximum bother and inconvenience for him; not that he was not used to this. Not that he did not consider it right and proper that he should be inconvenienced. It was, after all, what he was here for. Minimum consideration as he was bumped again. He turned to apologise but the trolley had already moved on. He had no idea who to apologise to. This confused him even more. Lost in the vast charnel house of modern life, he walked further in.

As he progressed he saw shops and signs. Huge posters of barely dressed women shocked him. But the men were even worse. Then he saw something familiar. Words. Slogans. Tight, compact phrases which rolled from the eyes, off the tongue and took up residence deep in the subconscious. Break your limits was one. That was from some years before, he'd almost forgotten it. He didn't really like it then. It smacked of imperfect bodily functions. But obviously it was before its time. The irony was not lost. The picture, however, he didn't understand. A man in a canoe? Hardly the place you would worry about a scent. What were they doing to his words? Then he saw another. It was buried deep in the crotch of a woman who wore, well, nothing so far as he could see. He was ashamed to look but the words called to him, seduced him. Just Be. He smiled. Swapping his glasses around he looked with his other eye. The lens was not quite perfect but he could see enough. Now he knew it was true. Both eyes had seen it. His words. Out here. It warmed him, gave him strength. Maybe there was hope. They were here to help, to urge him onwards, to prevent a catastrophe. But those pictures? He hurriedly replaced his glasses and strode further into the middle of the hanger.

The noise increased as he walked further and further into the building, searching, his eyes scanning the horizons, embarrassed that he made eye contact with so many people. He felt violated by this, that he had to be where so many others were. He could smell them all. Individually. But beneath the almost physical wash of sweat and breath and feet and vomit and food and coffee and beer and disinfectant, he could sense something else. Delicate hints of citrus. A shimmering haze of sandalwood. A vibrant undercurrent of musk and powerful shades of summer fruits. Beneath the violent aromas of modern man lay the sweet and delicate scents of nature. Captured, bottled and sprayed. An aromatic camouflage, an odiferous obscurant. A fragrant fence to keep out intruders; a bouquet of barbed wire. It was a pity that books never lived up to their titles. But did anything? He snapped out of his reverie and saw what he was looking for. A man. Dressed as if he were important. A security man. He strode up to him as purposefully as he could.

'It's my wife.'

'Excuse me, sir?' he spoke with none of the deference Winston had hoped for from a man in uniform, a public servant, but with the irritated tones of the man who had so recently cut his leg. It was all that he could do to stop himself apologising and walking off. But he was in trouble. He needed help.

'My wife. She's trapped in the car. We crashed, you see.' He paused. 'The fog.' Winston was almost stuttering now. The man looked at him, scanning him up and down before suddenly looking as concerned as Winston was.

'Where exactly, sir? I'll inform the emergency services. Don't worry, we'll take care of everything.'

'On the approach road. I had pulled off the motorway as, well, you know, woman's things.' Winston looked embarrassed. The guard hurried towards the exit, motioning Winston to follow him.

The man chattered into his radio as they both arrived at the doors and Winston found himself, suddenly, back in the fog which was so threatening, the fog which had threatened to deprive him.

'How long does it take to walk from here? Can you take me now? I understand if …'

'Three minutes and twenty-four seconds, at normal walking pace. If we break into a gentle jog, I would estimate two minutes and, let me see, twelve seconds?' The security man had stopped in his tracks.

'Is she badly hurt?'

'I don't know. She wasn't moving when I left for help. She wasn't wearing her seatbelt, you see. I told her to, but she does so like to live a little dangerously.' Winston stopped talking, cocking his head slightly to the side as if in thought before shaking it repeatedly. 'No, no, no.' The security guard looked at the small, scared-looking man in front of him who had seemed to drift off into another world as he explained in such a matter-of-fact voice that his wife was not moving when he had left.

'How long ago did you leave her?'

'Pardon? Oh, yes, let me see, it will be seven minutes exactly. In fifteen seconds. Not long. I was unhurt.'

'But your glasses?'

'A separate incident. Why, may I ask, are we waiting here?'

'The paramedics are to meet us here.'

12

'Will they be long? Only we may not have much time.' Now the small, insignificant-looking man was starting to assert himself. The security guard wondered how anyone wearing a cardigan could ever assert themselves, let alone get married.

'I'm not qualified for first aid. I have to wait. They'll only be a minute.'

'They've already been one minute and..'

'Here they are. Let's go. Follow us.' He motioned for the team to follow them and trundled off, at a gentle jog.

'Forty-three seconds. Turn left.' Winston was following now. The guard was large and unfit. Winston wandered how he had got the job, he was clearly not a man on whom one could bestow much responsibility, let alone trust. Trust your senses. He liked that. It had potential. He filed it. 'Over the road. There, that tree.' They had arrived at the site of the crash. 'There, you see. Two minutes and forty-two seconds. You should do some exercise.' The guard was breathing heavily, unlike Winston who spoke in the same calm, measured tones as he always did, unless he was speaking in public, or to a member of the public. His nerves seemed to vanish in the fog, as he called to his wife.

'Don't worry dear, these good gentlemen will have you out in a minute.'

'Fuck me.'

'I beg your pardon?'

'Sorry. Sir.' The sir was most definitely an afterthought. 'It's just, what a mess.' In front of him was a brand new, pillar box red Ferrari. And a tree. They were so closely connected you would think they were in congress.

'How can...' the guard started, then thought better of himself, and motioned to the paramedics. 'She's in the passenger seat. No belt.'

13

'Jesus'. The windscreen on the passenger side was crazed with the hazy, ribbon-like lines which appear after a heavy collision. The heavy collision between cranium and laminated glass. 'That looks nasty. What's her name, sir?' Winston looked confused again.

'Oh, er, I, Claudia? I'm not really sure.' He muttered to himself, going for the door as he did so. 'Don't worry, darling. Not long now.' He was starting to look distraught. The paramedic team moved in, one of them wrenching the door off its hinges. He stopped in his tracks.

'Sorry sir, there doesn't appear to be anyone here. She must have regained consciousness and wandered off. Very common in these types of crashes. Made a bit of a mess of the car, mind. No blood. Strange. Jesus. It stinks in here.' Winston ran towards the car, sobbing. He pushed the man out of the way, took one look inside, and fell to the ground, his arms on the door sill. He lay his head on the leather seat, inclining it to one side as the tears in his eyes began to affect his voice.

'I told you to put your belt on. I told you, but you wouldn't listen. Now look at you. Crushed and bleeding.'

'Sir?'

'My wife.' He held up the remains of a bottle. 'My beloved. I was so close. That's why we came out tonight. I knew I was going to name her. Oh, that scent. Wonderful, don't you think? Like the essence of violets combined with night-scented stock, crowned with, let me see, a slight hint of rosemary. But it's gone now.' He collapsed to the ground. Sobbing. 'I'm sorry.' The three men moved away from the prostrate form of Winston who was now starting to gibber unintelligibly.

14

the leper colony

Let me put it like this; if I am to prevent myself from being bowled over when I stand up, I must ensure that I swim as close to the shore as possible, so close, in fact, that my belly scrapes along the bed, before I stand up and begin to walk. That way the waves will only be able to lap gently and benignly around my feet. I did exactly that. I was goggled, but naked, and though the water was warm, the bed was littered with stones, indistinct but apparent in the disturbed and turbid water, sand kicked up both by my proximity and my flailing arms, which rubbed against my skin, smooth and cold. They made it difficult to pick out the shape. At least at first. But it was warm, and I soon realised that it was no stone; it was a knife. More specifically, it was one of those chunky, thick diver's knives with a thick, weighted black handle with finger grips engraved on it and a thick guard to protect the fingers from the indecently curving, almost scimitar-like blade which stands opposite a grimly serrated edge. Even beneath the shroud of the sand-infested water it maintained a faintly malevolent gleam. It was still contained within its holster; warm and thick rubber slabs wound up with webbing strips. An obscenity enclosed. Imprisoned.

As my head breaks through the surface of the water and I tear my limbs from the grasping fluid I see that the beach to which I have swum is deserted, bar a woman and a child. Young, maybe four years old. The woman is the same age as me, approximately, and she is also naked. She lounges indolently on the sand, the stones she has cleared from her resting-place lie in a small pile at her feet which are drawn up towards her chin, leaving long, invitingly languid lines in the still-moist sand. She props herself

15

up on her elbows, her shoulders attempting to make contact with her neck as she twists and squints through the steadily lowering sun towards me. All the while our daughter plays. Alone. Some ten yards away. With nothing.

I look behind me at the water I have just left as it laps at the footprints I have made in all innocence, wiping away the sand's memories, and can see that we are on the edge of a bay. There is a small island about five hundred metres away. I think I may just have swum out to it. But I am not sure. The island is covered in trees and shrubs; verdant and teeming where the shore we now inhabit is desiccated and lifeless. Except for us. She looks at me and I shake my head. No food. There is no food and there is no-one else. There is nothing. Nothing but us and stones and sand and water. I see some driftwood on the shoreline, a large hulk of rotting wood sitting amongst the flotsam of the sea's recent rejection and I pick it up, dusting off the caked sand and the mermaid's purses and the dismal seaweed. I attempt to make fire, frantically rubbing at it with a thin stick I have also recovered, palms pressed close together and burning hot as if in prayer, but the wood is rotten and wet, and crumbles as soon as any attempt to create friction is made. Though I have no idea why, I go once more into the sea, wading out into the bay until the water reaches over my waist; no longer afraid of the waves.

I am struck on my left side. No more than a dull thud. No pain, it is not even as if whatever has struck me is solid. I am not startled, and look down to identify my attacker. A plastic boat, inflatable. Capable of carrying maybe two children. On its edge there are two ice-cream sticks attached with brown parcel tape to the vulcanised hull. I peel them off and hurl them as far as I can into the bay. They drop, lifelessly, into the water some three feet from where I stand and begin to drift aimlessly, bobbing

16

like some sort of hi-tech cork on the swell. I return to the beach.

As I return, I can make out a wall of old brick and crumbling mortar at the back of the stretch of sand upon which we sit, some twenty yards away. Behind it there are buildings. Buildings which appear to have been deserted for some years. I wonder why I failed to spot them before, there was no fret that I recall, but now dusk is staking its claim on the horizon. There are the ragged forms of cars beside the buildings. Parked. Not so much parked as abandoned, though I can make out a T registration Rover. It seems to have something wrong with its left rear tyre. It's not flat, merely at a strange angle.

Through the gate in the wall walks a man. I look up at him as if it's the most natural thing in the world and he looks down at us as if we are the sole reason for his presence. He is disfigured, the right side of his face a shock of bubbling and erupting flesh, simultaneously drawing the eyes as it repulses the mind. I pick up the stick with which I had so recently failed to set light to anything and brandish it threateningly at him. He laughs, shouting at us that we were trapped; trapped forever in this colony. His colony. Then he runs away, feigning fear as I make a lunge for him but fail to carry it through, as if afraid myself that any contact, even the merest brush with the stick, may result in transference, infection, contagion. We decide to search the buildings, find a room and hide.

It seems like an old hotel. It is ragged and worn, yet again it seems deserted. The wallpaper is faded, old and mildly tasteless, though without being gratuitously offensive. We find a room on the first floor where we can bar the door and enter, drawing the threadbare curtains tight against discovery from outside. Our daughter seems to have got hold of my knife. She runs the blade against her flesh and makes to insert the point into

17

her belly. We stare amazed, transfixed by her behaviour and her apparent innocence until I am stung into action and strike like a benevolent serpent, removing it from her hands and strapping it, along with the holster, firmly to my right ankle, out of harm's way. As I removed my goggles after leaving the sea I have been naked, but am no longer. The sea gives me succour. She looks at me, petulant and annoyed, but says nothing. I open the door and venture out into the corridor, stick held far in front of me to prevent unforeseen contact. To prevent unforeseen infection. Unforeseen union. There are many doors along the dismal, dank corridors which now seem to be damp with the sea air, the carpet feeling like a thick matting of still-moist seaweed, as if it has followed us inside. I see the doors opening and closing and more than once I chase an unseen intruder from the vicinity of our hiding place. Back in our room, I look through the crack in the curtains and see two people approach the hotel. I decide to ambush them, to interrogate them. Discover our situation, bargain for our release.

I walk to the stairs slowly, taking care that I am not seen. I check each of the doors as I pass, making sure there is no-one behind them. The seaweed carpet is drying now and it tickles my naked feet and, satisfied, I walk up the stairs, deciding that that should be my hiding place; I shall ambush when they get to my level. I crouch down, stick in hand, metal stair protectors cold against my naked feet, carpet fronds and tendrils rubbing against my flesh, reaching up between the cheeks of my buttocks, and wait.

Soon I hear voices. From below. They are on their way, and they are talking. Talking about me. I clearly hear my name mentioned. Over and over again. I leap forward, confronting them on the landing with my stick and my fully armed ankle.

There is only one person now. I am sure there were two. But there are no doors off the stairs. No-where for the second person to go. They cannot ambush me from above; I would have seen them pass me. I concentrate on the one person who presents. A woman. Wearing a green smock coat. She greets me kindly, seemingly unafraid of my nakedness and my stick and my knife, and leads me into a long room, away from my family, and as I look back I see a pair of legs with your boots on, long, luxuriant black leather boots on, I see a pair of black leather boots with your legs inside disappear into the next room. I point this out and attempt to follow but I am ignored. I am wearing your boots. Your boots and nothing else. My captor has my knife. She has taken it and hidden it, taken it and hidden it without my knowledge. I realise I must be careful.

In the room I am watched by hundreds of pairs of eyes. They are laughing eyes as I walk with my captive captor in her green smock coat and me in your black leather boots and we sit at a table. They grin and point and shovel great big spoonfuls of beans into their mouths, regardless of whether there is any room left in either mouths or already bulging cheeks. I see the juice run down chins and hear the laughter grow and see the fingers point and feel my cheeks burn with shame and my crotch stir and I sit on my chair and rock gently backwards and forwards, my knees up to my chin, my arms encircling them cold against the black leather and my eyes buried downwards and worried about my wife and child and her pile of stones and she's playing with the knife and all I can do is rub my pathetic stick into the cold, sodden and rotting timber and wonder why there is no fire and jump over the waves and hide behind the mask and sit and rock and rock and sit.

Then I see you. Why am I in this place? I ask. And you smile and sit beside me and I see you are wearing your boots now. Why am I in this place? I said I would protect you, why am I in this place? You did protect me, you say. Now it is your turn, you say. And I look around me and all I can see are the rotting faces of my fellow prisoners.

nigel, prince of darkness

Zachary Vaughan leant his elbows on the pock-marked and drink-stained table and quietly inspected the tall chaser of beer, its sides rank with condensation, as it loomed arrogantly above its tiny companion; a shot-glass of dark, musty bourbon. He threw the bourbon back and lit a Marlboro, leaning backwards in the rough, wooden chair which tilted slightly to the left as if it had only recently had a hip replacement which hadn't gone exactly according to plan. As he exhaled he noticed absent-mindedly how the cigarette smoke seemed not so much to disappear into but combine with the damp and foggy atmosphere of the bar. It was a small, rough place, with little choice of drinks other than beer and bourbon; a typical mid-west blues bar. Its crowd was mixed, rough-looking and unforgiving but seemed to be awash with a sense of anticipation. Zachary had heard about this guy on the grapevine. It was said that he was good. Damn good. As good as Zack himself, some said. Now, Zachary knew that this simply could not be true, so he had come down to The Long House to give him a lesson in humility. It wasn't just that he was good, oh no, it was that he'd been telling everyone how he was The Greatest Blues Guitarist The World Has Ever Seen. Zachary knew this couldn't be true, if only because *he* was The Greatest Blues Guitarist The World Has Ever Seen. But people were starting to agree with him.

Zachary looked down into the swirling morass that was his beer as the man walked onto the stage and started to play a solo piece, the band respectfully allowing him to start off his set by staking his claim. Zachary would give him staking his claim. He had his guitar nestling close by his side, as always, the leather of the case gently touching his calf, sending an almost erotic charge through his body every time he moved like the less than innocent brush of a future lover's hand on a bare arm. He would wait until this upstart had said his piece. Then he would give him the signal. That 'my god I can't believe how good you are' look that steals across a musician's face when he is stunned and chastened by what he has heard. The callow youth would recognise it and, unable to resist, imperceptibly will Zachary to join him onstage for a jam; a duel. Now, the audience here knew Zack, so they'd love that. The upstart, however, might not be so thrilled with the result. Zachary thought back to the first time he'd pulled this particular stunt and basked in the warm, glowing feeling produced by the singular combination of recognising another's hubris and drinking one's own whisky. Then he looked up at the stage and the man who was laughingly being termed his 'competition'. Zachary was taken aback. This guy was good.

As his fingers caressed the strings, all the pain and sufferings of a lost generation seemed to pour out from the battered body of his '58 Strat: withering, stinging chords which alternately seduced and repelled the ears with their combination of sweet consonance and violent dissonance; coruscating, cascading lead lines which insinuated themselves into the soul with glassy subtlety whilst simultaneously penetrating the mind like hot worms of revenge, bitterness and gall, and all delivered with a tone as smooth as the smoothest bourbon yet as brittle as the glass shards of the argument-shattered bottle. This man was not a blues guitarist; he was the blues. Incarnate. The very physical and spiritual embodiment of the oppression of countless generations through the unrelenting misery of slavery and poverty. This man had the very water of the Mississippi Delta coursing through his veins - his blood surely a synthesis of this and rough, moonshine whisky - yet he bore none of the lineaments of the stereotypical blues guitarist. His hair was short and neat. He was clean-shaven and his skin was taut, tanned and healthy-looking. His suit was immaculate, cut superbly and quite plainly bespoke. He looked more like a successful lawyer than a musician. And he was white. Zachary tried to imagine his name. Blind Lemon Litigation. Jelly Roll Advocacy.

The guitarist looked at Zachary as he sat, slackjawed, at his table. He had seen this look before, it was the look of a guy who reckons himself hot shit, but is suddenly confronted with Aaron King; The Greatest Blues Guitarist The World Has Ever Seen, bar none. This was the time to catch his eye, get him onstage for a duet, a duel even, before he recovered his reason and realised that such a move would be suicidal for his reputation, a little like Kevin Costner's decision to act alongside Alan Rickman. As he drew his opening statement to a close with a series of outlandish suspended chords the like of which Hendrix had never even considered and the crowd went wild, throwing hats in the air, whistling, whooping, hollering, he threw a disdainful glance at the forlorn figure sitting there in front of the stage, looking as if he felt more alone than he had ever felt before. The man looked up and their eyes met with a savage intensity which, just for a moment, scared Aaron. It was as if this man hated him more than anything on earth, and that if he couldn't be better than him (which he surely could never be), he would have to kill him.

Zachary saw the fear in the guitarist's face as their eyes met. He knew that he, Zachary, was the only one of the pair of them who knew. The only one of the pair of them who had the slightest

23

idea. He stood up, and saw the guitarist onstage start slightly before his grin returned as Zachary approached the stage, his guitar case gripped tightly in his hand. The crowd noise gently subsided as Zachary slowly opened the battered, gig-scarred case and took out a weather-beaten '58 Strat. Left-handed. As he stood up and plugged his guitar into the nearest amp, the guitarist held out his hand and smiled. It was a lawyer's smile; the one where they show you their teeth.

'Aaron King.' He said, matter-of-factly.

'Zachary Vaughan.' Replied Zachary. 'Let's play.'

Aaron started off the proceedings with a twisted, two-note lick, not unlike something Freddie King might have played; taut, tense and with a stinging vibrato. Zachary played it back to him immediately; perfectly. To this retort Zachary added a Stevie Ray Vaughan style run; all pull-offs and attitude. Aaron played it back to him immediately; perfectly. The crowd, the very same crowd which had, moments before, been delirious with joy and an almost febrile excitement, were suddenly rendered as silent as the grave as the two guitarists traded note-perfect copies of each other's licks. This was no ordinary duel, they could hear that, and they didn't want to miss a thing. No-one took so much as a sip from their bottle. Cigarettes burned slowly down to the fingers and seared flesh unnoticed until they fell, exhausted, from soot-blackened hands. The guitarists looked and sounded like mirror images of one another, but it was impossible to tell which was the genuine article.

Suddenly they both stopped playing, and there was silence. A hush the like of which the bar never experienced, even when completely empty in the dead of winter. This silence was the true, deep silence that is qualified by potential. The potential for noise. The two men smiled at each other, but this time no lawyer's smiles; these were the warm, heart-felt smiles of recognition and acceptance. As one they played a gentle intro to a rub-shuffle and counted the band in.

As their fingers caressed the strings, all the pain and sufferings of a lost generation seemed to pour out from the battered bodies of their '58 Strats: withering, stinging chords which alternately seduced and repelled the ears with their combination of sweet consonance and violent dissonance; coruscating, cascading lead lines which insinuated themselves into the soul with glassy subtlety whilst simultaneously penetrating the mind like hot worms of revenge, bitterness and gall, and all delivered with a tone as smooth as the smoothest bourbon yet as brittle as the glass shards of the argument-shattered bottle. These men were not blues guitarists; they were the blues. Incarnate. The very physical and spiritual embodiment of the oppression of countless generations through the unrelenting misery of slavery and poverty. These men had the very water of the Mississippi Delta coursing through their veins - their blood surely a synthesis of this and rough, moonshine whisky - yet they bore none of the lineaments of the stereotypical blues guitarist. Their hair was short and neat. They were clean-shaven with taut, tanned and healthy-looking skin. Their suits immaculate; quite plainly bespoke. And they were white.

Forty-five minutes later, the crowd were reduced to a silently stunned, chastened congregation. Some were weeping. All knew that the thing they they had just witnessed, the thing they had just experienced, was something very, very special. These two players had improvised for three-quarters of an hour on the one tune, playing the exact same licks and chords and squeals and feedback noises as each other. Simultaneously. Without a pause or a mistake. Absolute perfection in the art of blues guitar playing. Twice over. They had not traded licks, but shared them. No matter what either of them had played, no matter how off-beat or unpredictable, the other played it at the exact same moment. After ten minutes or so of trying to outdo one another, they had simply allowed themselves to be swept away by the music and had played the deepest, most sublime blues the world had ever heard. Both Aaron and Zachary still thought they were The Greatest Blues Guitarist The World Has Ever Seen, and they were right. They were. Both of them. They looked at each other, smiling as the audience melted in dumbfounded approval and appreciation, and as one they left the stage.

Aaron sank back into his chair, sweat-sodden, and chugged the beer handed him by Zachary, but not after first holding it up to him as a mark of respect. 'You are one amazing player.'

Zachary nodded. 'You too.' Zachary handed Aaron his pack of Marlboro and then took one for himself before he lit them both, drew the smoke deep into his lungs and blew it into the swirling, misty atmosphere of what passed for a dressing room. Already the house band were playing up a storm, but somehow the atmosphere had gone - that cross between disbelief and absolute conviction which had gripped the audience had disappeared the moment the two men had left the stage.

'I don't know about you, but I almost feel sorry for those guys. I mean, imagine having to follow that.' Aaron said before grabbing another beer.

Zachary smiled to himself. 'How long ago?' he said. Aaron looked up.

'Oh, about three months. Down in Louisiana.' He paused. 'What about you?'

'Six, and it was here. You were a lawyer, right?'

'How can you tell?' Zachary smiled once more, a broad,

26

knowing smile. 'Oh, I see. You too. What field?'

'Contractual mainly, I worked for a lot of musicians. How I got into this lark.'

'I was libel, but the same area. Funny, really.'

'What?'

'Well. We both wanted to be the greatest blues guitarist in the world…' Zachary interrupted,

'That the world has ever seen. And in capitals.'

'Yes, absolutely. We both wanted to be The Greatest Blues Guitarist The World Has Ever Seen, so we do the obvious thing.'

'Exactly. Let's face it, most people would reckon we got a good deal.'

'Some would say we committed fraud. After all, whoever heard of a lawyer with a soul?' They both laughed. There was a pause while they both assessed their situation.

'The complete lying, cheating bastard.' They said. In unison.

'We really should complain. I mean, we are indeed The Greatest Blues Guitarist The World Has Ever Seen, but, well, we both are, and that doesn't really count.' Aaron said, scratching his chin. 'Zachary?' he asked.

'Call me Zack'.

'Zack. You're in contractual law.' He corrected himself. 'Were. Wouldn't the definite article imply a singular case?'

'Most definitely so, if you'll pardon the pun.'

'So there's no room for sharing joint honours?'

'Not so far as I can see.'

'Fuck it, let's sue the bastard.' Aaron said, jumping up from his chair.

'For what?' Zachary asked.

'Well, for our souls for one thing, and then compensation for the stress and humiliation caused. I mean, we can only lose. I presume you checked out the contract fully?'

'Watertight. If it wasn't for the definite article.' Zachary paused. 'You're right. Let's sue him.' Both men went silent. After all, it wasn't every day that you file a suit against the Prince of Darkness. Not least of their problems was how to get in touch with him. There was a knock at the door. They were surprised, as the band had stopped playing some time ago and most of the audience had left to spread the tale of the night they saw The Greatest Blues Guitarist The World Has Ever Seen. Both of him. The door swung silently open and in walked a small, nervous man with a squint. They stared.

'May I sit down?' He asked in a tremulous voice. They nodded their assent and he sat, took out a small cigarette case and lit up a cheroot.

'Jesus, it's you.' Stammered Zachary.

'Not quite, and I would be grateful if you would kindly moderate your language.' Said the small man with the nervous countenance. He looked the two men up and down. 'Oh, for pity's sake,' he roared, 'I can hardly walk around town with horns and pointy tail, now can I?' There was a flash and a slight smell of sulphur and the little man disappeared, replaced by a large, broad-backed beast which might have resembled a man if it hadn't been for the deep crimson colour of his skin, the fact that his lower body would plainly have felt more at home bounding up and down mountainsides and had the addition of a long, whiplash tail and two appropriately evil-looking horns. 'Better?' he enquired, menacingly.

Zachary recovered some of his poise first, and managed to stammer. 'Sorry, I didn't recognise you. And, well, it doesn't feel right talking to the Prince of Darkness when he looks like the third accountant from the left as you walk clockwise.'

のnigel, prince of darkness

'Well,' said the devil, 'you obviously have no idea of what, exactly, constitutes hell for most people, now have you?' He smiled, as much as the Devil can smile, and gently metamorphosed into a dapper, sharp-suited man of about fifty, powerfully built and with thick, black hair shot through with pure white. 'Now, what seems to be the problem?' He drew deeply from his cheroot, exhaling a thick, red smoke. And he smiled.

'Well,' Zachary started, 'it's like this.' He paused.

'Yes?' Inquired the Devil.

'Sorry. Look what should I...' he hesitated, 'I mean we, call you? Satan? Mr Devil? The demon formerly known as the Prince of Darkness?' He laughed nervously. Then less so when the Devil laughed along with him.

'Look, as demons go, I'm pretty reasonable, being all-powerful and so forth.' He smiled once more. 'And that wasn't bad. You've certainly got balls.' Zachary wasn't happy about the way that he smiled after he had said that. 'Close friends call me Nigel.' Aaron looked at Zachary, and Zachary looked at Aaron.

'Ok, er, Nigel. It's like this. We both signed a contract with you.'

'Indeed.'

'Guaranteeing us that we would, for the small price of the pledging of our respective eternal souls to you in perpetuity, become The Greatest Blues Guitarist The World Has Ever Seen.'

'And that you have, have you not?' The Devil, sorry, Nigel inquired.

'Well, yes and no.' Said Aaron.

'Yes and no?' Asked Nigel, stressing his conjunction to

29

indicate his inability to understand the statement. 'Are you or are you not The Greatest Blues Guitarist The World Has Ever Seen?'

'Well, yes I am.' Aaron paused. 'But so's he.'

'The problem being?'

'Well. The use of the definite article' Zachary began, but Nigel interrupted.

'Sorry, you're querying your contracts on the basis of semantics?'

'Absolutely. Though maybe more on the grounds of syntax, but anyway. What's the point of a contract if it fails to stipulate exactly what it is that you are gaining, and for exactly what price? Now, we both know the price; the pledging of our respective eternal souls to you in perpetuity. Sadly, you have failed to deliver on your promise, namely to make us The Greatest Blues Guitarist The World Has Ever Seen, as there are two of us, and we play exactly the same way. And we mean exactly, don't we Aaron?'

'Indeed we do. It's uncanny.' He looked at Nigel. 'Well, it would be were it not for your involvement.'

'Therefore?' Nigel asked, still calmly smoking his blood-red cheroot.

'Therefore you, the Devil, Nigel, whomever, have reneged upon your side of the deal. We cannot both be The Greatest Blues Guitarist The World Has Ever Seen; that would be tautologous.' Zachary looked at Aaron who nodded in appreciation.

'All right, maybe I was a little hasty.' Nigel started. And then smiled. Malevolently, obviously. 'But look, I'm the Devil, so you can both fuck off.' He smiled.

'So you're saying that the contracts are null and void?'

'Exactly.'

30

'Well you can fuck off then; you can't have our souls.' Zachary smiled. 'If you could just take them, there would be no need for this contract business, right? Or is it just a lark that you and God cooked up between you to see who's gullible enough to go for it?' The Devil frowned.

'All right, I'll get my people to look them over for you, I can't say fairer than that, now can I?' The Devil shrugged and looked over at the two men. 'I couldn't scab a beer off you, could I? I'm parched.' Zachary looked at Aaron, and Aaron passed him a beer. The cap flew off in transit. The Devil looked at them both. 'What, you think I need a bottle opener?'

'No. Not good enough. Seeing as we can't both have what we want, we want our souls back, plus some compensation for disappointment.'

'Compensation?' Nigel shouted, and small flashes of his previous incarnation crossed his countenance. 'I'm the Devil, for God's sake. I'm not giving you compensation.'

'That's how the law works. Trust me, I'm a lawyer.' Even the Devil raised a smile at this.

'OK. How about a sideways stylistic differential.' The Devil suggested. The two lawyers looked at him blankly. 'I'll make one of you The Greatest Blues Guitarist The World Has Ever Seen, and the other The Greatest Classical Guitarist The World Has Ever Seen. How about that?' They shook their heads. 'All right, how about a sideways medium-based differential movement, one of you can be, say, The Greatest Novelist The World Has Ever Seen?' Aaron smiled.

'Oh, and I suppose that means I'll end up writing Don Quixote again, does it?' The Devil looked at his feet. 'Touched a nerve, have I, Nigel?'

'I'm the Devil again, let's get that straight.' He snapped.

31

'There's no need to get shirty, devil or no.' Zachary grinned. 'I don't suppose Pierre Menard was a, how can I put it, client of yours, was he?' The Devil started to look a little stressed.

'Well, maybe he was, what of it?'

'I don't suppose he realised what happened to him, does he?

'No, I got Jorge to sort it out. Do you think I don't know my way around a library? Anyway, that's not really relevant.'

'Well, I think it is. Maybe he should be told, maybe there are others who've been conned; miscarriages of injustice if you like?' Zachary was on a roll.

'You're not trying to blackmail me, are you? You do realise to whom you speak?' The Devil looked somewhat surprised at the turn of events. After all, it was usually he who indulged in this sort of behaviour. 'I invented blackmail.' He stammered, indignantly.

'And very grateful we are for it, too. Of course we're not trying to blackmail you,' Aaron cut in, 'We're just suggesting that with a few alterations to your business practices, you can run a far more successful and watertight operation, that's all, and also trying to warn you of the possibilities which may occur should your little, how can I put it, marketing faux-pas become more widely known.' Aaron lit another Marlboro.

'Those will kill you, you know.' The Devil said, ungraciously.

'Well there's no need for that attitude, now is there?' said Zachary, suppressing a smirk.

'Look.' The Devil began. 'You guys. You just swan around playing the guitar without doing so much as an afternoon's practice, oh, it's only a soul and haha, he's fucked up the admin. Do you know how difficult it is to get good admin staff down there? Most secretaries and clerks go straight to heaven on the grounds that they've spent all their life in hell already. Hell's full of moody bastards with rampaging egos, all bickering and whining. Adolf wants his own apartment, away from Genghis, because he can't stand the way he smells. How did that man persuade a nation to do all those things? He's such a pathetic little prick. I mean, he should by rights, be upstairs with all the other pathetic bastards, but no, I've got to have him. His paintings are awful, too. Good job I've got Caravaggio to do all my interior design. The only decent admin guy I've got is Albert, and he's on holiday. I suppose Florence isn't too bad, though she's got a tongue on her like you wouldn't believe. Joe keeps airbrushing my best demons out of the end-of-year photos and Milhous automatically destroys any sort of record on sight. It's a bloody nightmare, and you wonder why I make a mistake like this? I'm not omni-bloody-potent, you know. I'm immortal, and if I happen to have made you both The Greatest Blues Guitarist The World Has Ever Seen in the same era, well I'm sorry. You can have you souls back. Fine. I'll get some more somewhere else.' He sank further down into his chair while Zachary and Aaron looked at each other in amazement.

'Look, Nigel.' Said Aaron. 'Let's go out, grab a beer, maybe a bite to eat. Our treat. Looks like you could do with a night off.'

The Devil nodded his head sulkily and started to get out of his chair.

'Oh, and we'll get back to you about our compensation for loss of life-long dream, as well.' Zachary added.

'Whatever.' The Devil said, and they all trudged out to Zack's car.

'Where do we fancy?' Aaron said.

'There's this little blues bar over on the West side. Should be hopping by now, especially as our exploits will be all over town, and it seems appropriate. What do you say, Nigel?'

'Whatever.' They climbed into the car and drove silently across town, the Devil sulking in the back seat, mumbling occasionally about what a bloody awful job he had and they should try being the Prince of Darkness for a while; see how they liked it. They arrived, got out of the car and were stopped at the door.

'No can do, boys, not dressed like that.' Said the doorman who was three hundred and fifty pounds of slightly smelly and greasy bad attitude with a cut-off leather waistcoat with 'Hell's Angels' embroidered on its back. Nigel stared at him. He sat down. Nigel was cheering up.

'Well, being The Devil does have certain advantages.' He said, smiling. 'I ask you, embroidered?' He continued to no-one in particular. 'Do they really think they'll make it? Oh no. They'll all go straight upstairs. Jesus wants them to embroider him a sunbeam. Stupid bastard. Imagine how embarrassed he'd be at the next meeting if it gets out that he tried to refuse Satan entry to his club?' He chuckled to himself, took out a small, black notebook and scribbled in it.

Aaron and Zachary found the idea of a chuckling Devil somewhat unsettling. As they walked in, a table suddenly cleared in the packed club, just to the left of the stage, and strangely enough, no-one tried to sit in it before the three men were there. They ordered beer and some nachos, Nigel giving specific instructions that his should be without jalapeños, and they sat down to their beers. Zachary looked at Nigel's cheroot inquisitively.

'What's that?'

'You really don't want to know.' Nigel said. They were aware that people were whispering and occasionally pointing, and noticed as the hum of anticipation gradually increased until the

34

room was at a fever pitch. A young man took to the stage and looked over at their table.

'Let me guess,' said Zachary, 'Pig Boy Grunt' and he and Aaron laughed, not noticing the young man smile at Nigel just before he started to play.

As his fingers caressed the strings, all the pain and sufferings of a lost generation seemed to pour out from the battered body of his '58 Strat: withering, stinging chords which alternately seduced and repelled the ears with their combination of sweet consonance and violent dissonance; coruscating, cascading lead lines which insinuated themselves into the soul with glassy subtlety whilst simultaneously penetrating the mind like hot worms of revenge, bitterness and Aaron and Zachary looked at one another, dumbfounded, before returning their united gaze onto Nigel.

Nigel blushed and shrugged his shoulders, sheepishly.

Nigel, aka the Devil; formally known as the Prince of Darkness.

black box

hardly a pumpkin

It had a been a long, tiring night. The guests were past the rowdy stage and had entered that quiet zone of semi-inebriate contemplation, huddled in groups around coffee tables and perched on the edges of sofas discussing the things dearest to their hearts, letting slip their Freudian neuroses and hoping quietly that the unwritten rule of no repercussions would apply to them just this once, as they themselves had applied it countless times, only to almost burst with the desire to share the sordid secrets gained at the expense of the latest failed relationship. Jim had just retired upstairs, dragging Sasha, his daughter by his first wife, unwillingly from the party. Sasha was nine, and it was way past her bedtime. As the last vestiges of twilight conversations drifted up to him, he could not stifle that feeling that now he was absent, the subject of conversation had turned to him. He reached Sasha's bedroom.

'Darling, it's late. Give daddy a kiss and then you really must sleep. Remember, mummy's coming to pick you up tomorrow, and I don't want you to be all tired, or she'll only complain.' Her mother was taking her for the week. Even after three years she was still seething that Jim had managed to get custody. She did nothing but complain and bitch about how badly he was bringing up her daughter. She did nothing but complain about how badly behaved she was now; how naughty she'd become.

'But daddy, I want a story.' Sasha always wanted a story, and what Sasha wanted, Sasha got. Just like her step-mother. Jim felt, on these occasions, that he was merely a servant to these grasping, manipulative women. But Sasha would smile and

37

his heart would melt. After, of course, the implicit threat to cry and sulk and pass on stories of ill-treatment and suchlike to her mother.

'All right. Just one. And then bed.' Jim was as stern as he could be. She took his hand and lead him into her bedroom, went up to her bed, pulled the covers back and got in. Jim tucked her in gently and sat on the end of her bed. The only light was from behind him, and it cast a wide, black shadow over Sasha as she lay, rapt with anticipation. He started.

'It was a dark and stormy night. The moon was full but obscured by clouds and the house creaked and leaked and the candles fluttered and spluttered as he walked down into the cellar. It was deep midwinter, and very, very cold. They had expected snow, and they had not been disappointed; it whipped in flurries at the windows and flew through the letter box only to melt gradually in the heat from the downstairs fire. Deep underground now, the old man was insulated from the raging weather, though he could hear the occasional gasp of wind and the banging of a pair of shutters which hadn't been secured properly. He was scared. He was scared because the night before it had happened again, and he knew that if he failed again tonight, it would leave tracks in the newly fallen, pure white of the virginal snow, bloody, raw tracks which would lead them to his door, just as they had led them to his father's and his father's before them; for they were the keepers of a great secret.' Jim moved from the end of the bed as the door swung shut and lay down beside his daughter, turning on her night light so that the room was now suffused with a ghostly glow. She looked at him, urging him on.

'What was the secret, daddy?'

'Well, I'm coming to that.' He made himself comfortable, and continued. 'They were not just the keepers of a secret, but of the results of a strange accident, which had taken place many years before, so many years, in fact, that no-one could properly tell when it had happened. It had been a dark hallowe'en's night, and it was a snowy, stormy night, not unlike this one, when it had happened. Legend has it that the son of the local squire had taken advantage of one of the local maidens, whose grandmother was reputed to be a witch, and that this witch had laid a curse not only on the son, but on the entire family. This curse was double-edged. It meant that the son would not only live forever, but that if certain instructions were not followed regarding his treatment, he would turn into a sort of demon, and terrorise the night much as he had terrorised that maiden all those years, maybe even centuries, ago.'

'What was the witch's name?'

'Well, the witch was called Yolanda, and she cast Yolanda's curse onto that boy. The curse meant that … but anyway, I'm drifting away from the story. The night before, the old man had failed to carry out his task, and the ancient boy had been turned into a demon, as had been prophesied, and had run riot among the neighbouring countryside. Luckily, no-one had actually been hurt, but bottles of drink had gone missing, yaks had been found the next morning shaved bare, and all manner of mischief had been undertaken. Tonight the old man was scared that he would fail once more. He knew that tonight there were too many people tucked up in their beds, easy prey for the demon should it escape. So he shut the door of the cellar and began his task. The boy was curled up on a truckle bed, much as you are now, and was wide awake, even though it was past eleven, and the evening was cold. His cat was curled up at his feet, fast asleep, but not purring. The old man sat by the bed and looked at his ancestor, older than him by decades, centuries even, but still as young as he had been that fateful, hallowe'en. The old man was tired and wrinkled and wore thick glasses and an unkempt beard. He stared at the boy as he opened his eyes slowly and they lit up the room with a soft, menacing glow, a fearful shade of red, as he awaited the spell which would keep him from harm.' Jim tried to suppress a yawn, and lay his head back on the bed, speaking now to the ceiling. 'The old man spoke. "It was a dark and stormy night …" You see, the old man was cursed such that every night he had to tell this child a story until the hour of midnight, the witching hour, had passed, and if he failed to keep his story going, then the child would turn into a demon, and wreak mischievous havoc upon the unsuspecting countryside.'

'Did he manage it, did he? Sasha asked, expectantly. But the only reply she got was a snore — her father had fallen asleep. She looked at his watch and smiled to herself. It read 11:58. Then she opened her eyes wider, and if Jim had been awake, he would have seen them glow red.

april fool

Jeremy was nervous as he walked into the restaurant, nervous that he would be found out, fearful that he may be unsuccessful, afraid that his well-laid plans would come to naught. He checked himself at the entrance, drawing a deep breath to compose himself before shaking the soft spring rain from his mop of dirty blond hair and removing his slightly damp jacket. He handed it to the doorman and walked in. Slowly. Calmly. A man in control. He knew that he was late, only five minutes or so, but late nonetheless. Late enough to impress the woman who was waiting patiently for him at the corner table, cradling a vodka martini in her left hand as she drew deeply from a long cigarette held in her right. She looked at him as he walked up to the table and smiled. They exchanged pleasantries and Jeremy simply indicated to the approaching waiter to provide them both with new drinks. He sat down. The woman sitting opposite him was older than Jeremy by maybe ten years, he wasn't sure. She stubbed out her cigarette and looked at him calmly.

'You're late.' She said, simply. Everything about her was simple. Direct. To the point. Everything except her intellect, her ability, and her position, that was. Jeremy found her strangely alluring. Usually he went for young, bubbly and somewhat vacuous girls. Girls who simply were not bright enough to challenge him, but sensible enough to admire him, to respect him. Whether he deserved it or not. Jeremy was not yet twenty five, but was already marked out for great things. At least, in his mind. He couldn't have a mere girl hold him back, interfere with his great plan. But this was a woman.

41

'Yes. I'm sorry. I got held up at the office. You know how it is.' He smiled. A winning smile that he had perfected some years back. It always worked. Jeremy had those angelic looks which some children of a certain class are born with, but instead of losing them as he hit puberty, they had simply carried him through. They carried him through life, if the truth be told. Arrogant as he was, Jeremy knew that this woman was far from being his equal. In fact, she was superior to him in every way. And she was also in possession of what he considered to be his immediate future. 'Shall we order?'

They ordered in silence. Good wine and good food. She was paying. This made Jeremy uncomfortable. Not the fact that she was paying. Jeremy liked his girls to be young, bubbly and vacuous, but also rich. They always paid. But Jeremy would make them pay, forget his wallet, insist on paying knowing full well that they would offer once more and he would eventually, and graciously, accept. He always promised to pay next time. There rarely was a next time, however; Jeremy used his girls and then replaced them. He never met the parents. Not unless he had been to school with one of their brothers, that is. But this woman, she was paying, and Jeremy knew that she was paying, and she knew that she was paying. This made Jeremy feel uncomfortable. There would be no polite refusals, no allow me's. Even the waiter knew that she was paying. He would give the bill directly to her. He had even waited after Jeremy had plainly ordered two more martinis until she had agreed to the order. Jeremy ordered. After asking her advice.

'So, Jeremy', she began, languidly, 'what do you see your future holding?'

'A glittering past.' He replied, glibly, regretting it almost immediately as she stared through him with gimlet eyes.

'Your proposal. It's, how can I put it, well, it's very brave.'

'I know.' He said. That was all he could say. His mouth had gone dry and he was desperately trying to resist the temptation to ask if he could bum a cigarette. What a way to make an impression, he thought. Finally he caught the waiter's eye and a pack was brought to the table. As he raised it to his mouth, she struck a match.

'Light?' She inquired.

He nodded in thanks and inhaled deeply, trying hard, but failing, to prevent a little splutter from escaping. He washed it away with his cocktail, and felt better. He felt, in fact, as if he had totally blown it. His big break. His dinner with the boss of one of the big names. His chance to impress, to climb the ladder, no, to get physically hauled up the ladder. It was too late. He'd blown it. He made a snap decision. Why worry. It's too late now. Enjoy the meal. She's paying. Try to seduce her. Why not. He's not getting the job anyway, may as well get a good story out of it. He had visions of himself at the pub, telling the story to his work mates: 'and then, would you believe, the bitch slapped me. I mean, as if I'd try one on someone that old.' They'd laugh, he'd laugh. He'd score points. Heroic failures of our time. It was the best he could do, and with a free meal thrown in, he could hardly lose. He relaxed.

Over the next three hours they drank good wine and ate outrageous food. He laughed, she smiled. He told a joke, she laughed. Jeremy started to realise that she may be in her mid thirties, late thirties, maybe, but she was still a very attractive woman. Powerful too, not just because of her position, but because of her poise, her confidence. He began to want her. Not only that, but he began to think that she wanted him, too. Maybe it was time to allow himself to be seduced, to be controlled.

43

Maybe he should be the trophy for a change, after all, they get polished every day and displayed for all to see. She definitely wanted him. Jeremy had a feeling for these things. Or so he liked to think.

After coffee they retired to the bar of the hotel. She ordered outrageously expensive whisky and showed him just how to savour it properly, rolling it around the palate and allowing the smoky, peaty flavours to suffuse what seemed like his entire being before knocking it back and feeling the deep, warm glow of alcohol burn its way into his soul. When she laughed she would throw her head back, oblivious to decorum, and a thick, throaty sound would emanate from what seemed to be the very centre of her. He stared at her neck; the lines were faint, but visible. They were lines that showed her life, her vitality. They were lines which showed exactly how much he had been missing with his vapid, skinny blondes. They had no life, no experience, no soul. He occasionally caught a glimpse of the top of her breasts as she bent forward, her blouse falling gently open to reveal her silk lingerie and the faint impressions of her nipples. She was a closed book to him, a promise of a night more wild than he had ever experienced before, a complete contrast to his willing, compliant and docile girlfriends. This was a woman who would control, order, and who would get what she wanted.

In the middle of one of her more ribald jokes, she suddenly stopped and stared at him, and her eyes lit up. 'Well, do you want the job or not?' Jeremy was struck dumb momentarily as her smile widened into a dirty, lascivious grin. 'Would you care to walk a lady to her room?' This was not a question. It was a command. She stood up, levering herself with a hand placed on his inner thigh, and sauntered gently off. Jeremy hesitated, before following. He could not believe his luck. He wasn't even going to have to try.

When he caught her up he placed a hand experimentally onto her shoulder, and she turned as she walked, and he swore later that he saw her lick a bead of sweat from her upper lip. As they waited for the lift he felt her hand slide slowly down his back and rest gently on the top of his buttocks. The lift opened and she pulled him in. During the journey from the lift to her room they kissed, her tongue urgently exploring, seeking his and pulling it back into her mouth. They reached the door and she slid her card through the key slot and they entered. Her top fell to the floor revealing her underwear as she unbuttoned his shirt, revealing the toned and hairless chest beneath. Now his hands were roaming, lifting her skirt and probing the inner recesses of her body. She was older than him but still in good shape, he thought, and she smelt divine; a musky mixture of money, whisky and sex.

She pulled him towards the bed and pushed him back onto it, and began to unbutton his trousers. He was almost giddy with anticipation. He was getting everything. Dinner. Sex. The job. She wrestled his Calvins to the floor and shot him one last, lustful look before burying her face in his crotch, teasing, tantalising and tasting him. He glanced momentarily at the calendar on the wall. It said April 1st. He surrendered. Completely.

Jeremy sat at the edge of the bed with his back to Jenny's indolently supine form as she lay, sucking hard on a cigarette and drinking straight from a minibar bottle. He held his head in his hands. He still wore his shirt, which was still unbuttoned. The rest of their clothes lay in blissful union on the floor, basking in the afterglow of cataclysmic congress.

Jeremy stood up, Calvins in hand, picked up his trousers, and

45

slowly dressed himself. Jenny smiled at him. A thin, cruel smile this time. Not the wide, lascivious grin which had earlier turned him inside out. This smile pierced his very soul. 'It's never happened to me before,' he said. And left.

don't disturb mr. evans

It had been the first rays of the sun falling on his face as they pushed their way through the flimsy materials of the curtains that woke him. It murders time, sunrise. That's what she used to say. What she had said to him the very first time they had watched a sunrise together, watched it together as the jaundiced disc that is the winter sun on the south coast drew itself painfully and rheumatically upwards, in a manner that could once have passed for slow and majestic, until it came to rest precariously on the horizon, its weak and vapid rays limping over the slate-grey sea off Brighton Pier. It murders time.

Joseph Evans had woken almost immediately, the cracked kiln of his memory being slowly fired as the morning rays tried to warm his face. It was a moment or two before he realised where he was, exactly. It had been the smell; that and the constant low murmur of suffering and disquiet that rumbled beneath the surface. It was only the very cheapness of the curtains that allowed the sun to penetrate to his position; he was four beds from the window, yet still the rays made it to him. Just as the feeble rays warmed his face, his feeble mind now turned over the scene set before it, and his feeble memory began to slowly calculate all the associations, combinations and connections to which it still had access. While he wanted to lie still and consume his past like some ruminant beast, chewing over every last detail, savouring those special moments through which he had lived, and there had been many, he knew, somehow, that he could not. It was not that she had left him almost as soon as the cancer took hold, the very strength which had first so

47

inspired him unable to countenance staying with a husband whose primary function in her life had been stripped out by the surgeon's knife and ravaged by the radiographer's ray; it was fear. It was the fear that she had felt when he had first told her, the almost physical sensation which takes hold of you, tunnelling deep inside the belly like an insidious worm; the fear of contagion.

That was why she had left. She had always been the strong one, the fearless one, but she was unable to stand and fight something she could not possibly defeat; her own fear. Her own fear seemed to be that his disability would reflect on her, that his inability showed that she was somehow less than a woman. It had confused him then; now it almost made him laugh. How pointless to be scared. Evans knew that he was going to die. And very soon. He had been able to smell death in the hospital ever since he had first been given a bed. There he was, a terminal case whose internal organs had suffered an almost continual round of mix and match for the previous five years, and he was placed in a ward full of geriatrics: colostomy men who leaked and farted and drooled and dribbled; demented pensioners left ignored and uncleaned by the apathetic and lazy staff. Evans was only forty-three, yet he had been put out to grass, left to die in this filthy ward. He looked up, knowing that however painful it may be, the sun could warm more than just his face if he moved.

At first, he had the idea that the wide, friendly face which smiled at him broadly was an angel; certainly he had never seen a nurse like this before, never even suspected that there could be such a person in this godforsaken place. But then, as the face reached across him and gently wiped his perspiring forehead he noticed the blue, surgical gown. No-one had stroked his forehead like that since, well, since whenever. His memory, along with all of his other intellectual faculties, those faculties upon which he had based his life, his livelihood, had been dulled somewhat by the chemotherapy. Emasculated, eviscerated and evacuated.

'I'm going to die. Soon, you know.' He said, and the face nodded gently, all the while wearing its smile like a badge. 'Would you take a letter for me?' It nodded again.

Evans started to talk. He talked like he had never talked before, he opened up in a way that she had always wanted him to, or so she had said as she finally left. That had been the real problem, apparently; not that she was scared, not that he was not. Not that she was seeing someone else, not that he was no longer able to perform. Not that she was embarrassed to have a cripple for a husband, not that he was dying. Oh, no it had been that he didn't talk about it. That had been the other thing. It was not just his cancer, the removal of what she seemed to consider his soul, it had been his reticence. She simply could not understand why he did not rage against the darkness; she took this as an almost personal affront. He could not understand why she felt he had to. After all, he was the one who could see it, not her. He was the one who was going into it, gently or not. Not her. Yet she was the one who raged. Now he talked. And as he talked, he thought of her face as she read this letter. He thought of the memories his words would stir as they took her back, back to Brighton Pier, back to where they first met. He would make her feel how he felt, see what he saw, think like he thought. All the while, the smiling face etched ever more steadily on a thick, white tablet of paper.

Slowly, steadily, Evans faded away. As he recounted to his wife all those things which he had always meant to say, but never had, the last vestiges of his life force drained away. He stopped, looked up at the face and took its hand. His eyes closed.

'There you are.' A gruff voice broke the silence and the smiling face turned around, away from the curtained eyes, as it was taken gently by the arm. 'I've been looking for you all over. I hope you haven't been disturbing this gentleman.' The nurse pulled the smiling face to its feet and started to walk away. 'What's that you've got in your hand?' he asked, pulling the tablet out from the grasping hand of the still-smiling face. 'Have you been stealing other people's paper to draw on again?' He pulled the top sheet off the tablet and quickly surveyed it, surveyed the mass of squiggles and dots and smiley faces which covered it. He screwed it up and threw it into the bin. 'Sorry about your paper, mate.' He said to the now rapidly cooling Evans, as he turned and walked away, the smiling face gripped tightly by the upper arm. 'He does this all the time. Right nuisance this one is, aren't you?' he said, speaking loudly into the face as they walked away.

As the two men walked away, another nurse walked in and drew the thin curtains sharply back. The clouds had rolled in, and it was starting to rain.

christian soldiers

It started with a slow, rhythmical throbbing. Just behind the left ear, about two centimetres into the meat of his cortex. Jeff slept increasingly uneasily as his head began to beat slowly in time, each unsteady flush of blood increasing the level of toxins in his grey matter, each systolic wave allowing them to seep ever deeper. Had he been conscious, the room would have begun to spin, and within a minute or two he would have been holding onto the bed to prevent himself from falling off. Had he even made it to bed, of course. Jeff lay in a crumpled heap in the middle of the living room of his cramped flat, which was perched precariously above a dry cleaners on one of the less high streets of his middle-sized, midly interesting market town in the midlands. Everything about Jeff's life was middling. That's why he drank. A desperate attempt to choose any road but the middle one. Jeff didn't have mid-life crises, he had mid-week crises, and this week had been no exception.

His recent affair with Linda (why are these affairs always with someone called Linda? And shouldn't that be Lynda, with a 'why'?) from the meat-packing factory had ended in disaster when he had shat himself in bed after a particularly heavy night. Lynda was not amused. He could see her disgusted face now. He could see the brittleness of her hair - she dyed it, even though she was a natural blonde. Brunettes have more fun, she said. He could see the way she'd looked at him as he crawled out of bed, as if she'd stepped in something. Not entirely accurate, of course: she had rolled over onto something. Lynda didn't see why she should have to have a boyfriend who shat himself.

Jeff tried to say it was something he ate, it had never happened before and that he really loved her, but it was useless. Probably a good thing, if he had actually thought about it. He'd only just got rid of the crabs she had given him. It had put him off meat for a week. Well, not quite a week. More like four days, but the Thursday night kebab was so tempting and, well, they didn't do kebab meat at the factory, so that was ok. Ok, it was longer than a working week these days. Jeff was on short time.

Jeff's left eye opened and his right arm felt instinctively down the back of his trousers, which were half off. It had become a sort of habit. A kind of insurance. His left arm, paralysed under his slumped body, failed to provide any sort of assistance in lifting him from the floor so he lay there, blood pumping, head spinning, wondering what the fuck was going on.

'Get ta fuck.' He spat. 'No fucking way. Bastards.' He was trying to shout, but it wasn't working. Half of his face was paralysed. 'It's only eight a fucking clock.' He thought he said, but it was probably merely internal. 'Christ, I feel rank.'

There was a violent crash, high-pitched and intense, and it hit his brain like a tidal wave of gravel, pitching up behind his eyelids and scraping his corneas, trying to find a way through the delicate tissue of his bloodshot and yellow eyes to the more delicate tissue of his swollen brain. 'Ah, ye bastards.'

Onwards marched the Christian soldiers, marching as to war. Marching as to the battle of the ridiculously useless musicians. Oddly enough, for all his foibles, Jeff had been quite a talented trumpeter in his youth. An incident with a trials bike and a bagful of evo stick when he was thirteen had done for his embouchure, however, and his talents now only occasionally surfaced. This was one of those times.

'Jesus, ye cannae even play in fucking tune, you useless pile of cunts.' He pulled himself a little more upright. His head span increasingly. 'I'll do a deal with ye,' he said, to no-one in particular. 'I'll give the whole fuckin' lot of ye a lesson in how to fuckin' play your fuckin instruments if ye'll just FUCK OFF.'

With the cross of Jesus, marching on before they marched on, as tunelessly and loudly as ever.

Another walloping great crash of the crash cymbals shattered the dull repetition of the big bass drum and one of the trumpets split into tritones, quite spontaneously.

Tiring of his attempts to drag himself upright, Jeff slumped back down on the floor. This was quite reasonable, however, as the previous evening he had consumed six or seven pints before decamping back to a mate's where he had polished off the best part of a bottle of whisky. He had crawled into his cramped flat only a couple of hours previously, and was more pissed than hungover. It had merely seemed that he was hungover, when the band began their interminable crawl up the not-so-high street. This was not, reasoned Jeff, with what was left of his intellectual function, fair. He deserved to have a hangover, yes. Absolutely. Lying in bed on a Sunday morning not wanting to move because your head hurts so much and because you're scared you'll either shit yourself or throw up was all part of the game. Hell, Jeff had even listened to the Archers, that everyday story of folky cunts, as he called it, because he felt too ill to turn the fucking radio off. He never had worked out why it had come on, but hey.

This, however, was entirely unfair. The Salvation Army were so bad, and so loud, that he was getting an extra hangover when he should have been enjoying being pissed. Unfair.

'It's no fuckin' fair.' He shouted, to no-one in particular. 'You cunts have no idea how good it is to be drunk, and how fuckin'

53

awful it is to be hungover. To give me one without the other is no fuckin' fair. If only you fuckers could have my fuckin' hangover, just know what it's like, you'd no wake me up on a Sunday fuckin' morning with your evangelical shite.'

Jeff swore some more, but it simply made him feel worse, and seemed to make the band louder, and to play even more out of tune. It was painful. Plus they only seemed to know one song.

Onward the Christian soldiers marched.

Then, something happened. There was a crash. From the cymbal again, but this time different. As if he'd fallen over. Jeff knew he'd fallen over because he'd heard the muffled words 'get up, you stupid cunt' waft gently upwards and into his strangely clear head. The mists were missing. The spinning ceasing. His nausea abated just as he heard retching from down below. He stood up. Perfectly. And went to the window.

As he walked over, without so much as a wobble, he heard the clang of brass on concrete. He spread his arms wide, palms on the grimy glass, and pressed his nose to the window. He started to laugh.

Beneath him, he saw the funniest thing he had ever witnessed.

He could see the drum master throwing up into a flowerbed, his cap tumbling off his head into the spray of vomit. Two of the brass section had dropped their instruments and were rolling about in the middle of the road, to all intents and purposes indulging in a good, old-fashioned, bar-room brawl. The leader of the band had simply fallen into an ignominious heap in the middle of the road and was laughing as he tried to restore order. There were men crying, men fighting, and lots and lots of swearing.

Jeff, laughing so much he could hardly stand, summoned up his sinews and stiffened his blood, and called the police.

'Yes, there's a disturbance outside seventy-four the high street. That's right, the dry cleaners. I mean, I wouldn't normally call, but it is eight in the morning on,' he choked back a laugh, 'God's day and, well, it seems as if these miscreants have had rather a lot to drink.' He paused. 'No trouble at all, officer.' He said.

Jeff continued to drink a lot. Sometimes his friends noticed that he never seemed to get drunk, but mostly they were too pissed.

black box

bandwagon

Harriet Alison Wayne is a feisty celebrity chick, a landscape consultant, more of a Prada Gardner than your average Charlie Dimmock: three-time UK free-style feng-shui champion, she utilises exotica such as Mongolian nose-flute bands to create her oh-so-desirable exterior 'atmospheres' - she calls it 'mindscape gardening'. This is no ordinary celebrity: HA Wayne has her immaculately manicured fingertips on the pulse of polite society. She is the demographic queen, desired by millions, emulated by millions more, and paid still further millions on a regular basis. Harriet does not so much live in the society pages as gives the pages society - a far cry from her impoverished childhood in rural Ireland. Her house has its own column in Hello, her garden shed and garden one in Homes and Gardens: she has a ghost-written thriller in the best-seller lists, shares in OK and a one-of-a-kind Porsche lawnmower. With all this fame, however, comes pressure, and this pressure leaves inside Harriet a deep-seated emptiness. She has spent her life trawling through her peers in search of that special someone, but for what does she seek? The one? The perfect profiterole? The Ideal Home? Will she ever find it? Through the hilarious device of text-messaging the reader's phone with easy-to-download 160 character chapters and unmissable emails, Bandwagon traces her attempts to answer her deep, inner yearning by commissioning a TV show in which ten contestants are slowly whittled down — one is voted off each week by a telephone poll — to find her ideal partner: Harriet has put her faith in demotics and the taste of the great British public. After all, without them, she would never have been able to start the trend for Givenchy water features currently sweeping the home counties. But what will her line of famous exes, including interior designer Laurence Latter-Day Byron, fellow gardener and literary giant Auden Titfield, chef Richard T Carr and the front-row forwards of Harlequins RFC make of her volte-face? Will they sell their story to the Wimbledon Inquirer in a fit of mass jealousy and expose her sordid past? Does the mysterious roman hold the key?

Peony looked quizzically at her companion, chardonnay half-guzzled as the sun's rays beat down mercilessly on the collected celebrity hoard. What was the collective noun for a group of b-list celebs? A gag? A schmooze. A smarm? Maybe a retch. Geraldine Thompson scratched the side of her more-than Roman nose in thought. Not very deeply in thought, it has to be said.

'Well?' Asked Peony.

'Darling, I think you're marvellous, and your name will sell just about anything these days, but isn't this a tad, well, auto-biographical?' Geraldine swilled her chardonnay around the faux-crystal before tipping it into the nearest plant-pot. 'Ok, more like aspira-graphical.' Peony swallowed back the urge to berate her.

'They say everyone's first novel is autobiographical, don't they?'

'Yes, but, well, I'll put it to the board. I'm sure they'll agree without so much as a sniff. After all, there's plenty of fiction there too. You may have to change some of the names, however. You know, to protect the insignificant. I just think you'd be better off with something a little more, how can I put this? Lightweight?'

Geraldine glided into the distance, slipping her arm around

her husband of three months, the ex-gangster Freddie 'Fingers' Farquahar, his soubriquet earned as a result of his predilection for using the amputated fingers of victims, be they alive or be they dead, as the raw materials for his carefully carved chess-sets. Fingers and Geraldine had met at a garden party the year before, a mere month after his release from Rampton, and immediately started work editing his record-breaking first novel, *The Long Finger of the Lawless*, a tome which concerned the death-bed confessions of an East-End gangster. That these tales could only loosely be defined as fictional was confirmed when a fingerless skeleton was discovered, as predicted, inhabiting part of the M25. Freddie had been heard to boast that one of his many escapades included the sale of a vast volume of out-of date concrete to the contractors. The skeleton came to light, fossil-like, as great scabs flaked off the bridge supports. Naturally, there was no evidence to link it to Freddie. The ensuing increase in sales of *The Long Finger* prompted more than one member of the literary circles from which Peony sometimes drew silent solace to comment that it was plainly an ancient, if inspired, publicity stunt. Maybe, they wondered, the corpse was that of a far-sighted PR consultant. If only. Peony hated Geraldine. She knew that her novel would be unlikely to get off the ground now, even if it were published. This was, of course, because Freddie had been with Peony when he and Geraldine met. Introducing one's slightly more notorious half to one's putative commissioning editor, only to have not only him but one's putative publishing push stolen from under one's very perfect nose was a little too much to bear. Peony looked around for another pot-plant she could disfigure. The rank wine she had consumed and her previously empty stomach were conspiring to upset the equilibrium of any poor, innocent, lime-loving plant that was unfortunate enough to find itself in her path.

'Are you quite all right, Peony my darling?' Inquired a plummy voice from over her left shoulder. It was Laurence, and he had spotted her looking somewhat over-like the plants in whose company she seemed to spend so much of her spare time these days. Since Freddie, there had been a string of celebrity lovers, just like poor, lonely Harriet, but none had quite hit the mark. Peony was twenty-eight, and starting to feel a little like she was over the hill. Last year's news. Grade c. Small c, to boot. Her mindscape needed a little more than a mere tidy-up, she felt. Maybe digging up and starting again.

'Never better.' Replied Peony before vomiting into the appropriate flower-bed, her bent frame hidden by Laurence's flounces. 'I don't suppose there's anything to drink around here, is there?'

'If it's any consolation,' started Laurence, 'I'm none too fond of young Freddie, either.'

'Oh, it's not Freddie,' Peony said, straightening herself up before sluicing the taste of gastric fluid out of her mouth with a quite acceptable Zinfandel, 'it's bloody Geraldine.'

'Geraldine?' Voiced Laurence, 'I thought you two were thick as thieves?'

'That's just it.' A pause. 'There's meant to be a sort of code, honour amongst media whores. That sort of nonsense. So when your partner in crime steals your criminal partner, not to mention your best means of generating publicity yet, it rankles just a little.'

'Hmm.' Said Laurence, in that ever-so slightly camp manner that he had perfected. He was the Scotsman on the label of coffee and chicory extract. Just without the skirt. Ready? Aye, ready. His flag was often at half-mast, however, just as it had been when Geraldine had been whisked from under him, almost literally, by the fingers himself. 'How's the book coming along?' Anything to distract himself from dwelling on that afternoon.

'Buffers, I'm afraid. She'll "Put it to the board" on Monday.' Peony knocked back another glass. 'And we all know what that means. Peony Malone: Out of contract.'

'They can't do this to us,' said Laurence, 'I mean, we're … we're celebrities. We have the right to be heard. The public need to know our deepest inner fantasies. They need more than carefully managed borders and beautiful dado rails, moroccan bordellos and expert flash-frying. You weren't going to name me in your book, were you?'

'Good God, Laurence, you're not still moaning about your flippin' bordellos, are you? Get with the programme, darlin'. It's Palestinian retro refugee chic this year. All the rage. You wait 'till you see what we're cookin' up this arvo. Pukka it is.' It was Richard T. Carr, chef extraordinaire and quite flavour of the month, if only because he was unafraid to use all manner of bizarre ingredients in his quest to bring back simple, home cooking to the masses. The masses of Notting Hill, that is, and preferably the masses who can say to their personal chef, "Enrico, Jasper and I think it would be positively divine if at tonight's party we could chow down on some Venezuelan Cassowary burgers flavoured with Mescal pickle and Sycamore nut pesto. For fifteen. Chop chop." Perfick, he might have said, had not that particular catchphrase already been copyrighted.

Peony was, it must be said, at a low ebb. She watched Laurence and Richard indulge in one of their epic battles. And in the blue-blood corner, we have Richard T. Carr and the faux Cockneys: in the mauve with just a hit of vermilion corner …

Mr Laurence Latter-day Byron with his fabulous flouncing fringe. She slipped into the background, her exit covered by the great Auden Titchfield himself, gardener to the stars for a night crowd, as he swept all before him. She was glad to be free, the only reminder of her celebrity self being the cackle of the evil triumvirate behind her. They were planning yet another TV show. This time, however, it was to be all-encompassing. Having selected some suitably d-list celeb, Laurence would re-design their kitchen and dining area, which would melt seamlessly into the garden designed by Auden, the fruits of which would be sautéed to within an inch of their lives by Richard. All they needed to do, they felt, was convince Peony to wave her particular magic wand. An image of her sitting down in a large leather armchair asking a be-couched perennial to tell her about its childhood flashed before her eyes. The conversation darkened as Geraldine piped in, suggesting Fingers as the ideal host for the show's inaugural outing. Peony silently considered the legality of explaining how to create a fool-proof shallow grave on the show's first outing before slipping behind the marquee. It wouldn't be long before the charity weakest link. All this for one paperback, she thought. If only.

'Freddie Fingers. You are the weakest link. Goodbye.' The Tannoy raged. The audience politely applauded. Freddie took the walk of shame. Not for the first time in his life. After all, he was almost expelled from Eton and had been rusticated twice from Kings. It had become clear during the quiz that he was more interested in inviting Anne's censure than actually answering any questions correctly. A charitable soul would consider that he was merely joshing when he suggested that the first man on the moon had been Jules Verne. A less charitable soul would have considered that he lived up to the hype and was, to coin a phrase, plain thick, but with that veneer of erudition truly thick upper-class people often have, just without the in-bred earlobes. The true cynic would have suggested that to win would be seen as arrogant, whereas to get voted off in the middle would have been a little pathetic. Better to make it look like everyone wants you out of the way, and give them a reasonable excuse for doing it. That's PR, darling.

'Personally, I don't know what all the fuss is about,' purred Freddie as the cameras were trained on him after the 'walk of shame'. 'I'd rather be voted off first than last, and Anne is such a pussycat. Beautiful hands, too...' He walked off into the faux Appalachian log cabin which housed the toilets where only the most sharp-eared of celebrity spotters would have heard the slow rip of his flies being undone, a low gasp and the dull thud which followed, some ten minutes later.

'Well, what on earth, Peony my darling?' Richard had been shocked back into his usual accent, the Sylvia Young chef-school training mask slipping for a split second. Stress. It always had this effect. Peony choked back a laugh as she visualised a moment from their all too not-brief enough affair. It was always at the moment of truth, so to speak, when Richard would come out with something along the lines of, 'Dicky, my old chap, my old chaaap,' before rolling into the corner of the bed and sobbing quietly to himself. Peony knew that at such times he missed his nanny.

'It's, well, it's Freddie.' Stammered Peony. 'He's had, well...'

'An accident? Yes, I can see that.' Richard peered a little closer. 'My, he wasn't such a big boy, was he? So that's why they called him fingers.' He paused. 'Dead, I suppose?'

'Oh yes.'

'And what do want me to do about it?'

63

'Well.' Peony began, ' you know how Procne avenged the rape of her sister…'

'Oh, I see. Well, why not.' Richard smiled as he began to whet his filleting knife. 'I imagine a nice ham or two…now, how to tenderise them.'

Richard T. Carr smiled to the camera as he beat down repeatedly with his tenderising mallet. 'I've soaked these fillets in lemon juice and pineapple juice, 'cos they're both, like, natural tenderisers. It's the enzymes, you see. Now I'm bashing the hell out of them.' The serrated head of the mallet made deep, rich thuds as it tore into the flesh. 'This is the best fun. Pukka work-out, too. You see,' Richard was starting to sweat a little, 'with good meat that is too fresh, y'know, hasn't been well-hung, you need it to be nice and tender before you can cook it.' He looked down at the array of flat fillets in front of him on the three-foot wide chopping board before hurling his patented wide-boy grin at the camera 'T'riffic.'

'The trick with roses,' began Auden, 'is to get a good blood and bone meal feed down. There's nothing like it for big blooms. Blood and bone. It doesn't matter where it's from. You see, the rose is a greedy plant, and it likes nothing nothing better than to show off how much it has drawn from the soil. So give it plenty of nutrients, and it'll love you for it.' Auden beamed.

'Now, for the coup de grace, so to speak, I'm going to take these wonderful sheets of thin muslin which I sprayed earlier with a dark red dye. It's sort of like a hippy tie dye but without the S&M factor.' Laurence smiled as he tossed his luxuriant locks camerawards. 'It's the random pattern of streaks which filter the sunlight just so that I love so, so much. It gives a room that bordello feel …' Laurence twirled his fingers around the bottom of the curtains, holding up the pale weights which he had threaded onto the stained muslin. 'Of course, if your stamina deserts you, you could always use the curtain weights for a game of knucklebones ...'

'So,' Geraldine began, walking slowly towards the camera which in turn panned gently towards her, 'let's walk through the space and sample the delights our celebrity panel have selected for us.' She sashayed up the wooden steps to the decking. 'Here we have a bunch of the most beautiful, blood-red roses.' She leaned conspiratorially towards the camera, and whispered 'don't tell Auden, but it isn't really blood meal which makes the colour, you know.'

'I've arranged the rose just so to enable the easy egress of those restless souls which can so easily destroy the equilibrium of a living space.' Peony was following Geraldine, speaking to her own camera. 'It's all a question of karma gardening equals calmer gardeners.'

'And next,' butted in Geraldine, a trifle over-anxiously, 'we enter through the, hmm, still a little damp, Laurence, streakily dyed muslin curtains into what could almost be a harem room.' The camera followed her face, watching as her nose twitched instinctively as she walked into the room.

'Of course,' continued Peony, 'fragrance is vitally important. To lay claim to the full feeling of security in a room, especially an earthy and, dare I say it, Laurence, visceral? room like this we need thick, earthy scent. Anything to take you back into the mother's womb, back to nature. I have found that hanging game can achieve this quite well.' Laurence smiled and bowed his head just a little.

'And, finally, we enter the kitchen, where Richard has whipped up a quite astonishing feast.' The camera swung over the table-top, dripping with delicate rolls and elegant kebabs,

'Is there a sort of Turkish feel here, Richard?' She took a kebab and sniffed it ostentatiously, her nostrils drawing in the rich, heady scent of rare meat and rosemary and the camera cut to her face just in time to see the dilation of her pupils, and she tore into the meat with an almost erotic fervour.

'You see,' continued Peony, 'in the right space, with the right lines and the right scents and the right energy flows, food can be as sensual as sex, biting into a kebab almost, dare I say it, like biting into a lover's willing flesh ...' she paused as a bead of sweat broke out on her upper lip, 'like biting into a lover's willing flesh,' she repeated. Slowly this time, and almost inaudibly.

'Good god, Richard, this is divine.' Geraldine was in ecstasy. 'It's almost like cannibalism, it feels so wicked. If only Freddie were here. He'd love this.'

i talk to the wind

I'm going to let you in on a secret. How it all began, so to speak. Now, I've never told anyone this story before, so you'd better pay attention. It really is how it all began.

It must have been thirty years ago. I was at school. I come from a reasonably well-off family, as you know. My mother was not a well woman. So far as I recall, my father simply muttered that eternal catch-all 'women's troubles' whenever I ventured to discover the cause of her violent mood swings and the episodes of tearfulness which were monsoon-like in their intensity and abruptness. It was not until ten or fifteen years later that I discovered their real cause. But I digress.

The net result of my family's position in society — that of an easy, inherited solvency — and my mother's pending nervous breakdown, was that I was to be packed off to a boarding school. I can't have been more than nine or ten years old. Timid, unimaginative and quite unprepossessing I was. Not, I'm sure you'll agree, ideal boarding school material. You are thrust, like the most innocent of lambs, into a world where almost everyone has known one another since they were young, maybe as young as six or seven: a cut-throat environment. So. Three years after all the cliques have been formed, all the pecking orders have been established, along I roll. This would not have been such a problem were I able to assert myself, thrust myself onto the situation, tame these unruly mobs of young boys, break up their cliques and re-write their rules. Timid, though, that's what I was. You'd hardly think so now. Just another one to be pecked way down the order. And pecked I truly was.

The school was situated deep in the countryside, in an old, slightly stately home which resembled nothing so much as a dowager aunt, a sort of Havisham Hall, all dressed up and decked out years ago for an occupant who never made it back from the plantations, or wherever the money had come from. The house had been falling into a state of gentle decrepitude which was accelerated when, sixty years after being built, and without so much as one even unofficial lodger in the interim, the school moved in. No real possibility of it being haunted, other than by a Dickensian, proleptic ghost. Things were not entirely organised there. Nothing was ever quite taken care of. After all, it never had been; merely finished and left to rot quietly. We were parasitic, and as a result the house, the grounds and the social fabric of the organism that was the school always came second to the boys who inhabited it. A close second, it's true. Second nonetheless. In some ways it could claim to be a true democracy, inasmuch as it truly was the will of the people that ruled, though those oligarchs who held the reins of power would never have suspected. And while it was more of a general won't than a general will, Rousseau would still have been proud. We even had a lake and a boat in which balmy summer days would be wished away.

The house had a mind of it own from the very beginning. It seemed to change its floorplan at will, and for weeks after my arrival I would be confronted with rooms and corridors and seemingly secret passageways in which I would get hopelessly lost before, miraculously, I would appear once more outside a common room or dormitory: never, however, where I had expected, and rarely where I wanted, to be. Sometimes I would turn out of a room into what can only be described as a Möbius lobby. Attempts to escape were futile, and for all its grand size and labyrinthine complexity, there seemed to be no place to hide from the prefects who would come on a Saturday night, worse the wear after their rum and cokes or the pints of local bitter which lay heavy on their breath, and would proceed to torture drunkenly the younger boys. That meant me, primarily. It was under their blows that I learnt the value of forbearance. I soon realised that if you were silent the pain would subside more quickly as they tired of you and sought another, more vocal victim. To this day the smell of stale beer makes me sweat.

Was it here that I first discovered my sensitivity? My talent? My gift? Was it in the teeth of such adversity that I turned inwards to find a higher truth, a greater purpose? In a manner of speaking, yes, but if you are looking for the key to my success, you must delve a little deeper. These contacts I make, these words I can chose, these words I repeat. They all come from the same source: I talk to the wind. I feel like Blake, confronted by the ghost of a flea and compelled to draw it, to share its form with an ignorant, wastrel world. I feel like Isaiah, my unclean lips purged by the righteous coals from the altar of the almighty, yet those words which I utter ignored by all who hear them. Or am I Jonah, forced against my will to travel and speak words which will not come to pass? I am all those things, all those people. I talk to the wind and the wind talks to me, reveals to me, and with its words I heal the sick and comfort the bereaved.

We were arranged into dormitories. Nothing strange about that. Also, we liked to fight. We liked to combine our strength and invade our neighbours, groups of ten-year olds rehearsing for the infinitely more bloody combat that was to come. There is truly no need to abandon children on an island to discover their power, their spite, their rancour. It was a wonder that we didn't invent our own national flags. Deprived of any meaningful way in which to acquire actual territory, we concentrated on other ways of exerting authority: pain and humiliation. Pain we inflicted through the simple, if traditional, method of hitting the desired victim with a pillow. That's right; pillow fights. Normal pillows were, however, entirely insufficient for our purposes. A normal pillow is only used for play-fighting, the type that leads inexorably to its logical chiasmus: ama, non pugnare. We created a more sure weapon through the simple expedient of replacing the soft goose-feather inners with tightly rolled woollen blankets of the style the army used to use and which, I am reliably informed, are not so much disposed of at the end of their useful life, but rounded up and shot: we called them atomic pillows. So. Objective one was the causing of pain. Into the dormitory of death strode the six. Blankets to the left of them. Blankets to the right of them. The second objective was always to demolish the beds. In fact, for those of us with a more malicious and farsighted bent, this was always the first objective. Pain is transitory, and within the confines of the school rulebook, there was little one could do to make it last longer than a few seconds: any obvious bruising would lead to instant dismissal, and, in any case, was a little unsubtle for us. Humiliation was part of the pain inflicted by our pillows, it is true, but what we really wanted was to force our victims into confrontations with law and order. These were confrontations they would always lose. So, we would demolish their carefully tended beds.

We were kept under strict discipline. We made hospital corners that would shame a nurse. These took time. Thus, to destroy a well-made bed was to strike a severe blow to enemy morale. A poorly or hurriedly-made bed would attract all manner of censure the next day. So we stripped beds. We hurled blankets and sheets out of windows. Adding stains to the sheets was another cause of great embarrassment. A stain, no matter how caused, would lead to the imposition of rubber sheets. These would not only be paraded into the dormitory just before lights out, that is, when all the pupils were getting into their beds, but were monumentally uncomfortable and made a noise when you moved. This was humiliation at its greatest. That the victim had not actually wet the bed was irrelevant, if not part of the point. To cause an unfair punishment was an achievement in a world where censure which was deserved was worn as a badge of courage. On more than one occasion, a boy so tortured would begin to wet his bed once the sheets were installed. That these sheets were of a similar texture and smell to army groundsheets, if a little thinner, caused some of the more sensitive boys serious problems in later life. One, I believe, even committed suicide as a result of having wet himself while on exercise with his men.

Once, in a rare example of united action, we joined forces with the inhabitants of another dormitory to effect the total and abject humiliation of a single individual. These children, I trust you understand, were and are world leaders in waiting. We had manoeuvred the bed, still occupied by the slumbering victim, through two sets of doors and half-way down the main stairs to the staff assembly point - we were going to initiate a fire alarm not long after his installation - before he woke up. Close. No cigar. Yet what we really wanted to do was to strip beds of bedding. It was this activity which drew me to my fate.

My line of work is communication. Just like its more obvious forms, I am a facilitator. I cannot do the work myself. Like the telecom company which provides the lines to link lover to lover or child to mother, I straddle continents. The difference, of course, is that my clients only ever need to talk to themselves.

71

The continents I straddle are internal. I am the Colossus of Rhodes on a synapsal scale. When I leave this plane I pass through the true pillars of Hercules. People say that the past is another country. I believe that the self is another person. It is only through calm and consistent internal dialogue that we can overcome the barriers that make us what we are.

It was late one night. Dark. Winter. Not as cold as it could have been. Not as cold as when the condensation on the inside of the dormitory windows froze. Cold enough, however, that you could see your breath by moonlight. Small puffs of spirit leaching out into the free world. There was to be no dorm raid tonight. Something rather strange had happened. The previous night, two beds had been denuded of their carefully organised coverings. Blankets, sheets, pillows. All found the next morning on a heap on the floor. The beds were on opposite sides of the room, so it was conceivable that the same person had stripped each one simultaneously, grabbing hold of the bottom end of the covers and pulling. A difficult task, but not beyond some of the boys. There were two characteristics of this attack which set it apart from others, however. The first was that no-one admitted to having carried it out. This was particularly strange, as there was never any point in doing such a thing unless the victim knew exactly who is was who had perpetrated the insult. This in itself was the cause of much speculation. Speculation was a new thing when it came to such events. The questions who or why had never before been asked, and thus could not easily be answered. The second, and far more serious, problem with this attack was that the occupants of each bed had been exactly that at the time: in occupation. Not only had an anonymous individual caused two boys untold irritation by successfully destroying their beds, but they had managed it while the victims had been asleep. Now, top covers, blankets, pillows and bottom sheets. All in a pile at the bottom of each bed. How? This was the cause of much consternation.

As I have already mentioned, there was not much in the way of nascent spiritual activity within the building. To the best of my knowledge, not one individual had ever died within its walls, let alone suffered the privations necessary to cause any sort of haunting. After lights out, it was a common pastime to discuss such things, as I was particularly interested, not least as I occupied a bed under a window which had a reputation for causing, though no-one, of course, could say how, the expulsion of its incumbent from the school. After the 'event,' we began a discussion of the occult. This discussion was exactly the same as all other schoolboy discussions of the occult. It took place after lights out, from the safety of our beds, and was carried on in hushed, reverential tones. I suppose such discussions are, in later life, replaced by flirtations with friend's wives. It was one pointless ghost story and 'creepy' occurrence after another. Very bland and dull. Then, as if by the powers which we discussed, the door slammed shut and the window, under which I was snugly wrapped in my perfect hospital corners, followed suit some two seconds later, having taken an almost perfect dramatic pause. This was, of course, taken as primae facie evidence for a truly supernatural entity: the school's first. Not only that, but it had chosen our dormitory in which to demonstrate some little part of its power. It did, of course, also serve to solve the mystery of the stripped beds.

It was the next night when it happened, when I knew finally what I was, what I was to become, and what fate held in store for me. As I have said, hospital corners were the order of the day. To avoid having to re-make the bed each morning

73

(assuming that no-one had attacked it the night before) one could slide gently in and never move, sleeping on one's front. This was my general method. I was then, as now, an insomniac. I would lie one my front, covers hard against the back of my neck, for hours, simply pondering. Part of the reason for this insomnia was my abject misery: I hated the school so much that to be asleep was nirvana, yet the very moment of sleep would, no matter how involved and lucid the dreamstate, bring almost instant morning. Thus I was involved in the insomnia of delayed gratification: I would savour every moment of agony before the bliss of sleep. Thus I found myself awake at three or four in the morning most nights.

I felt suddenly cold, and the hairs on the back of my neck tried hard to stand up, hampered though they were by my bandage-tight sheets. And then it happened. I felt a hand, cold, hard and bony, on the back of my neck, gripping the sheets and blankets hard, as if to pull them from my now shivering body. As they pulled, the pressure of the covers was released and I spun around, eager to confront my attacker. After all, I was plainly the victim of a new type of assault, the type which had occurred just the other night: the silent attack. No wild, whooping rush. No headlong assault. Just stealth, guile and surprise. If the victim woke, there would still be ample time to escape, and insufficient light to identify the attacker. I, however, was fully awake, and would discover the perpetrator of this vile, cowardly attack.

As I spun, my eyes alighted on a pale face atop a body shapeless as if wrapped in a cloak, as the bony hand which had so recently defiled my skin and caused a cold, cold sweat to break out retreated in what later turned out to be super slo-mo. The face was still and unafraid, and I did not recognise it, even though it was gently illuminated by the pale and sickly moon as it shone through the window. We were both still and silent. I, alone, was slick with clammy sweat and awash with fear. Mouth dry, I mouthed a word. The bony hand was raised to the lips and I was transported into another world.

Where I was taken is still a mystery to me, but what I was shown is not. I was shown my future, and yours, and how to commune with the wind as if it were my brother. I was taken on that journey from which few, if any, return. That same journey, I suspect, that Isaiah, Dee, Blake and maybe even Crowley had travelled before me. And since then I have tried to use the power that was placed in my hands that night for the good of all. That night, I saw the face of God.

Trenchard breathed out slowly and calmly before taking the glass of water from the glass table in front of him: he lifted it to his lips and drank. He leant back into the lush leather armchair and smoothed his hair, the grey now reaching around from the temples onto the crown, clasped his hands together and smiled. A beatific smile. The smile of the justified.

'Well, Trenchard,' started Parkinson, before losing his way in his own sentence, on his own show. 'That certainly is an amazing story. And from that meeting has come everything?'

'Absolutely. That one night, all those years ago, has enabled me to cure, to comfort, to truly empathise with all of my, well, I can hardly call them clients, now can I?'

'No, I suppose not. Now, I know this isn't normal practice, but I'm a little lost for words. A revelation like that deserves another, reciprocal gesture. I'd like to ask whether any member of the audience has a question they'd like to ask of Trenchard Cleats, clairvoyant, spiritual counsellor and, dare I say it, prophet?' he looked at Trenchard who nodded approvingly, and the audience, which had sat rapt for the past few minutes, slowly drank in that they, too, were able to make history. A few wavering hands were held aloft, as if they were simple puppets, their strings pulled eagerly but unconvincingly. Parkinson pointed at a gentleman. 'You in the dark suit, have you something to ask Trenchard?'

'Well,' he started, 'not so much ask but tell.'

'Really,' said Trenchard, 'do continue.'

'Well,' continued the man, I thought I'd seen you before and, well, Trenchard isn't your real name, is it?'

Trenchard smiled, if a little thinly.

'Don't worry. That secret's safe with me.' The man seemed nervous now. 'Do you remember me?'

'I can't say that I do,' started Trenchard. 'Ought I?'

'Well,' said the man, 'it was a long time ago, but I was the boy who woke up half-way down the stairs.'

There was applause and laughter. Parkinson leaned over to Trenchard and whispered something before speaking to the entire audience, 'How splendid. Friends reunited indeed. Has anyone…' He was cut off.

'That wasn't what I wanted to say.'

'Oh?' said Parkinson, 'do continue.'

'Well,' the man's nerves were getting to him now. 'It's just that the 'face of god seems a little over the top to me.'

Really,' said Trenchard, before sipping once more on his water. 'If you had been there, if you had seen what I saw, I assure you…' The man interrupted once again.

'But I was there, you see.' He said, slightly irritated now. 'You were always going on about ghosts and seeing spirits and how your stories were better than anyone else's and, well, after the bed incident, I decided to get my own back.'

The audience was silent: the wait for the riposte grew longer.

'What are you trying to say?' Asked Trenchard.

'Well,' started the man.

'Oh, for heaven's sake,' Trenchard almost shouted. 'Would it be too much to ask that you manage to begin one sentence, just one, without a "well"…hmm?'

The man was quiet. Then he said, simply, 'it wasn't the face of god you saw. It was mine.'

black box

turning, point?

The migraine which seized him was not merely unexpected in its arrival, but it appeared to have taken the majority of his modifiers with it as it left. Once, he might have anthropomorphised his affliction, portrayed it as the cranial housebreaker gaining entrance with the aid of a jemmy through the left eye, rampaging through his temporal lobes upsetting his carefully compiled and filed work stores in search of easy pickings before leaving through the left temple with a bag of adjectives slung on its back, the crushed remains of innumerable choice adverbial clauses lying in its wake. Perhaps a handful of metaphors carefully, cunningly mixed. A couple of well-turned phrases, pointedly up-ended. A simile, soiled.

He was broken. It had happened while he had been listening to a new patient, a complex case including a turning round of his expectations, a turning down of her advances, and a turning in on himself. She had been curious, an extreme version of what was now as mundane for him as it would be terrifying for anyone else. The migraine had hit him like a hammer. He shut down.

It was almost two days before he regained consciousness. He heard a soothing, emollient voice, soft and breathy in his right ear. His left, he later discovered, had been bleeding, the fall beginning the process of his turning deaf. He turned his head, pointed to the damaged ear, and lay it gently on the floor. The voice simply continued, unabashed, unabated, unhinged.

'You fucker.'

'Hang on a minute.'

The thought that everything wasn't quite right did a little more than cross his mind as it ploughed through a whole series of questions, twisting as it did so and turning, point after point falling by the wayside as thought made tangible knocked them from their narrow perches …

He began to understand, to sense, to feel, to be confusion.

'You little fucker.'

The voice again. Soothing, emollient, but with undertones turning savage as it pointed out yet another failure on his part.

'Fuck off.'

It was the best he could manage under the circumstances. His mind so clouded … so very clouded. Occluded. Obscured.

'Now you just stay right there …'

He began again, feeling his tongue slowly returning. Slowly returning to the point where he could contemplate … contemplate what? He heard a fast clacking sound, somewhere between a wasp's buzz and the clapping of a clockwork monkey, and felt a faint prickling on his forearm. He forced his right eye slowly open. The light he was expecting, the stinging, searing pain he anticipated never came. There was a faint glow coming from his arm, an iridescence which cast a blue-green haze, picking out the fine hairs which covered it and currently stood on end. As his pupil slowly opened itself, allowing the faint light in, the formless glow assumed a familiar shape.

The shape's familiarity was merely generic, as sat upon his forearm was a beetle of a type he'd not seen before. Quite large, but even in the gloom possessed of a depth of black he'd only seen at the plant, in the great slabs of silicon from which the chips were made, the chips which held everything: data, memory, consciousness. Identity. The chips which had been embedded in the brain stem of every citizen. The chips which facilitated the continuous observation of every individual. The chips which were a little less reliable than they ought to have been. The chips which it was his job to re-programme when they went wrong.

His patient was young, perhaps twenty years his junior. She was blank. Denuded. Naked, if only internally. She had been found wandering one of the lower levels in expensive clothing. After an interlude of what was laughingly called 'employment', she had been returned to her rightful place, assuming you ignore the fact that due to her lack of any actual identity they had no idea what her rightful place was. She was the worst case he'd seen so far. Normally his patients retained a certain amount of data, but she, she had none. She was a true nobody, an unperson.

He saw the beetle, its back to him, raise its wing cases slowly upwards, the iridescence increasing, casting shadows. But it failed to fly away, and instead began to turn, and in turning point its wing cases towards him. Then, the iridescence began to take shape, and the cases no longer simply glowed, but displayed ... the shape was one he recognised. It was her. His patient. Her photograph. Her data. It was her. Then the images flickered, died, and a new image presented itself to him. He recognised this person, too. His own face stared back at him. He knew, now, exactly what had happened. There had been no entry through the eye, no metaphorical thief had removed his ability with words. It had been a real entity. And it had merely sat on the back of his neck.

'Fuck.'

The voice again. Soothing, emollient, soft and breathy.

There was a sharp report and a stinging pain in his forearm as shards of beetle penetrated his skin, impelled by the hand which had crushed it. Which had united his patient and he.

'I don't think you ought to have done that,' were the first words the patient uttered.

the old man and the sea

He preferred the blunt simplicity of New York. Walk. Don't Walk. It was simple. Here, however, the red man simply recommended that one remained stationary. Jaywalking was not a term the populace of North London understood. Lionel tutted under his breath, shaking his head imperceptibly as a young mother pushed her child between two parked cars and into the road. The screech of brakes, the scream, the shouting, the cunting this and cunting that, and Lionel knew the child's fate. It may have been wrapped in blankets to guard against the cold of November, but there was nothing that could be done to protect it from the sheer stupidity of its mother.

'What you lookin' at, heebie?' Cried the woman, stick thin and gaunt, spitting her hatred in his face.

Lionel didn't reply.

'Well fuck off then, yid.'

She had seen the shake of the head and maybe even heard the tutting, but in truth she was simply deflecting her guilt onto the nearest available hate figure. Lionel didn't much mind. He wished for a better class of hate, however – the vitriol he received from such insignificant, idiotic people was habitual hatred. He much preferred the opprobrium of the educated. It seemed so much more proper. Being despised by those for whom the pushchair was an implement designed primarily to stop traffic for their benefit was almost embarrassing.

Lionel was somewhat past middle-aged, and at 5 feet 3 and weighing sixteen stone, he was hardly what one would call a fine figure of a man. He limped slightly from the gout which

83

was his primary inheritance from his father, and carried a cane to support himself. Winter, to Lionel, was something of a double-edged sword. The cold suited him, as he would sweat and wheeze in his suit during the summer, but the occasional patch of ice made him wary of walking too far in one go.

The green man lit up, and Lionel walked slowly across the road, ignoring the cyclist's expletives as he almost barrelled into him after ignoring the red light, and the cars which thought that when the lights flashed it was ok to edge threateningly towards the broad, behatted figure as he traversed the final few yards to the pavement.

He walked to the park's entrance, and held the gate open for a woman pushing a big, old-fashioned pram. Nana Goldberg was the daughter of an old family friend, and greeted Lionel warmly.

'Shalom, Lionel.'

'Shalom. Beautiful day for a walk, Nana. How is your dear father?'

'Not so well, Lionel, not so well. He must visit the doctor again this thursday.'

'More tests? Ay.'

'More tests. You off to town?'

'To the bookstore. I have some business to attend to. Regards to Manny.'

They parted. Lionel carried on walking. Past the empty pond. Past the derelict play area, avoiding the dogshit which peppered the pavement. As he looked up he caught sight of them. The three youths who had almost run him down on the pavement earlier in the week. He had shouted at them. They spat in his face and cycled off, laughing. This time they were sitting on a bench, smoking and drinking cider, their bicycles sprawled over the pavement in front of them. The two boys leaned back aggressively, arms and legs apart, and he approached. He heard one of them hawk. He heard him spit. He stopped. The mass of sputum landed a foot in front of him. He began to walk on.

'Not so mouthy now, eh, old man?' Sneered the elder of the two. The girl sat next to him pulled a line of chewing gum out of her mouth, winding it round her finger and then starting to chew it again. She had her other hand on the youth's thigh, just below his crotch.

'Yeah, stupid old fucker. Not so mouthy now?'

It was this lack of imagination that he deplored more than anything.

'Can you boys not think of anything more original?'

'Wot you fuckin' say?'

'I said, can you boys not think of anything more original?'

'Piss off, cunt.'

They laughed.

'You see, that's where you go wrong. Petty, foul-mouthed, pig-ignorant child that you are, you'll be in prison by the time you're old enough to vote.'

'Who d'you fuckin think you are, fucking jew boy? Fuck off back to your own country.'

'Ah, would that I could, would that I could.'

Lionel picked his way through the bicycles and carried on walking. He heard the sound of breaking glass behind him. Raised voices.

'Didn't you fucking hear me, yid fucker?'

Lionel carried on walking. The boy suddenly appeared in front of him, his bike skidding round and coming to a stop in front of him.

'I said, didn't you fucking hear me, yid fucker?'

Lionel stood still.

'I'm sorry, I'm a little deaf.'

'You're fuckin thick, that's what you fuckin are.'

'Now why don't you go back to your bench and drink some more cider?'

'Because I've drank it all, cunt. You give me all your cash and maybe I will.'

'Maybe?'

The boy put his face directly into Lionel's.

'My dad says you fuckers should all be sent to fuckin Yidland, let the arabs fuck you all up.'

'He sounds like a thoughtful man, your father. Known him long?'

'Don't you fuckin take the piss, or I'll fuckin cut ya.'

The boy took a paring knife out of his pocket and waved it in Lionel's face. Lionel doubted he had ever cut so much as an apple with it before.

'Now fuckin give me yer cash. My dad says you lot are fuckin minted. My dad …'

'Your father certainly has a lot to say for himself

The boy was beginning to go puce. He pressed the knife into Lionel's throat, just where his too-tight collar met the increasingly saggy and sallow flesh.

'Ok, ok. I'll give you my money already.'

Lionel found it helped if he spoke like a comedy jew. It always seemed to diffuse the situation.

'Haha. Listen to the pathetic cunt!'

Lionel reached carefully into his coat's inside pocket, and pulled out a calfskin wallet. The boy snatched it from his hands, tore the notes out of it and threw the wallet to the ground.

'Pick it up, yid.'

Lionel did as he was told. He had to get down on one knee to do so. As his hand reached out, the boy's foot clamped down on it.

'Call it the yid tax.'

He laughed. Spat on the ground and walked off. Lionel turned round to watch his antagonist. The girl hung off her hero's belt as he swaggered off. The second boy pushed the two bikes.

'Disgusting. I can see their bloody underwear.' Lionel said as he levered himself up off the ground. A blackbird burst into song in one of the bushes. The sun, which had been hidden behind clouds, burst out and bathed Lionel in its glow.

'And the Angel saw the ass … Well, I'll probably find him dead tonight on the way home, overdosed on heroin. No loss.'

Lionel walked for half an hour. Along the canal, through the shopping centre, and eventually to the row of shops that was his destination. The bookshop had been on this corner for as long as anyone could remember, and in its time had always supplied something more than just reading matter to its clientele. It was dark and a little dingy. It was difficult to make out people's faces, let alone the book titles in the rows of close-packed shelves.

Lionel pushed the door open. It was a little stiff, but gave in as he applied more pressure. A bell positioned above it rang out as he did so.

Lionel looked at his watch. It was 11.13. He walked through the shop to the back, lifted the trap door in the counter, and stood by the till. He picked up a bunch of orders and began to flick through them. The doorbell rang out once more and a ravaged looking man with sunken eyes walked to the desk.

'You've been holding a book for me.'

'Oh, yes, of course. Mr, er …'

The man hesitated.

'You're not the usual man.'

'No. He's ill.'

'I want the usual man.'

'He's ill. Mr …?'

'Smith.'

'Ah, Mr Smith. A first edition of The Old Man and the Sea. A delightful addition to any collection.'

'Yeah. The book. And hurry.'

'Of course.'

Lionel reached under the counter and brought out a large packet. The man began to open it. Lionel interrupted.

'Not in the shop, if you please.'

'Whatever,' he grunted. He began to turn around.

'Oh, and Mr Smith?'

The man stopped and looked at Lionel.

'What?' He sounded aggressive.

'I have a message for you.'

'What?'

Lionel reached into his inside pocket, brought out an automatic pistol with a silencer, and calmly placed a round in the centre of the man's forehead.

'We don't like your sort, Mr Smith.'

Lionel took the packet, checked that all the money was there, and placed it in his coat pocket. He pulled the body out to the back of the shop and disposed of it. Then he walked home. In the park, he passed the youth lying on the pavement in a pool of his own vomit.

'Each to his own.' He said.

And walked on.

a short, dark season

Pras Tata pulled the De Havilland Gypsy Moth sharply to the left, banking steeply as the Irrawaddy River unfolded beneath him. The late-afternoon sun was still strong and the day still hot, though Pras had noticed that fifty kilometres or so to the South the sky was heavily overcast, a huge bank of thick, dark cloud blotting out the sun, swathing the land beneath in a shadow which seemed to be advancing across a clear, abruptly delineated front. It was maybe a little early for the rains, but Pras gave thanks. South was the direction the Japanese planes would come from, so the dark skies increased his chances of getting in and out of Burma without incident as the rain he assumed accompanied them would discourage the Japanese from flying any missions not absolutely necessary. Beneath him, however, the land was still firmly gripped in the hot season's dry and chapped fist. It was only when he became airborne that his heavy clothes and tight leather flying mask had ceased to be severely uncomfortable. On the ground the prickly heat would start within minutes of his dressing for flight, turning his entire body into a seething war-zone as it ran up his arms and down his back, searching out unaffected areas and invading. Many times he had found it necessary to explain to the European pilots that he, though a 'native', was not immune to this seasonal curse. They, in turn, either took his suffering as further evidence that his Parsee's light skin signified European descent, or simply refused to believe him.

Now, however, his discomfort was relieved. The open cockpit of his aeroplane kept him in a permanently cooling breeze which, in any other climate, would have left him insufferably cold. As the aeroplane slowly levelled out to follow the path of the river he felt free in a way he never did when grounded. Pras liked nothing more than flying in the hot season. In the air he had all the advantages of the clear yet vaguely hazy atmosphere which gave everything visible a delicate light blue tinge, without the disadvantages of the stifling heat and dust below. During peacetime he had flown over this area many times, and delighted in the wide vistas of lush green and dust brown which the plain set before him. Now things were different. He was not looking forward to the monsoon which would be arriving soon, turning the ground below into a sodden quagmire, and turning his flights of freedom into unpleasant, uncomfortable and dangerous battles with the weather. These missions were already quite dangerous enough. He wasn't sure what he feared most; the Japanese airforce or the disaster which would come with the monsoon.

Beneath him the wide river gleamed gently in the sun, looking more like a benign and soporific snake than the large, fast-flowing and dangerous waterway it was and he followed the progress of the various barges of the Irrawaddy Flotilla Company and the native dhows as they struggled upstream towards Mandalay, away from the Japanese. It was a scene of almost unnatural calm, the area immediately surrounding the river lush and verdant, the procession of boats almost indolent, almost denying the fact that there was a war, there was panic, that there were columns of refugees fleeing for their lives.

He was flying his second mission of the day. For the last month he seemed to have spent most of his waking hours in the air, filling his tiny plane with assorted refugees, and, where possible, meeting Jerry Osbourne, or at least collecting his

90

bound-up rolls of film which, after they had been carefully sealed in tubes, he would deliver to the offices of the Washington Post on his occasional flights to Calcutta from his base in Chittagong. Jerry had been following the plight of the refugees; walking, riding and hiding with them, all in the cause of journalism. Pras had last seen him at Magwe, almost a month previously. He had landed late, and Jerry had finished off his last roll by lining up the four refugees Pras was collecting under the wing of his plane. They had looked almost comical; two women, one with a small baby in her arms and one holding the hand of her daughter, a child of four, maybe five. Jerry had insisted that they hold hands. Their luggage consisted of one suitcase, one folded-up sheet full of clothes, one teddy bear, one doll, and a chamber-pot. Jerry was pleased with the image, and the Washington Post had been, too. Pras' Gypsy Moth was only designed for three, one of whom was the pilot, but the children were small and, thankfully, so were the women, so their ride wasn't too uncomfortable.

Pras was suddenly struck by the realisation that the ominously dark clouds he had seen earlier; that he had given thanks for because they provided him with excellent cover; that he feared because he thought they had been the oncoming Monsoon; that had provided an almost figurative representation of the Japanese advance, were anything but. They had been smoke. They must have come from the oilfields that were twenty kilometres North of Magwe, which meant that either the Japanese were closer than he thought; maybe they had advanced as far as Yenangyaung or even Chauk, or that the British were setting light to them, to deny their riches to the advancing army. The Magwe airstrip itself had been overrun by the Japanese some four or five days previously. He remembered

91

the last time he was there; he had left in a hurry. The plane had been losing oil but it was vital to return to Calcutta before dark. Though he expressly asked the engineer to check his sump he had neglected to, and, time pressing, Pras was forced to take off with his gauges low, hoping and praying they would make it. He remembered the faces of the two husbands left behind as he took off, the engine coughing ominously, and wondered what had happened to them, whether they were still alive, and whether their evacuated families had any inkling of their fate. That was also the last time that he had seen any Allied aircraft flying in Burma which weren't concerned solely with evacuation. Two Hawker Hurricanes stationed at Magwe had left just after he did, scurrying away like beetles towards India to try to protect the cities there from the Japanese bombers. The remains of the force had been destroyed a few days later by a massive Japanese attack, apparently in retaliation for a successful British raid against them. To fly in Burma, at the front, was tantamount to suicide now. Pras knew it was starting to get too close for comfort.

He was to meet Jerry at Nyaung U, a small airstrip some ten kilometres North-east of Pagan. He would follow the Irrawaddy's stately progress until it ambled slowly to the right. Then he would cut inland for a few minutes and hook up with the journalist. He was, according to the garbled message Pras had received, travelling with a Red Cross convoy, and should have arrived by the early afternoon. Pras could afford to wait for about an hour if he had as yet failed to show up, before he would have to leave. He would be able to squeeze a couple of refugees in as well. He knew it wouldn't be long before these trips would become too dangerous, as the Japanese were pushing further and further towards the heart of Burma, and soon their airforce would control the skies absolutely, not just at the front, and each extra trip he made then would very likely be his last.

He was now only a few kilometres South of Pagan. This was one of the most famous areas of Burma, resplendent with over four thousand temples, pagodas and stupas, in various states of decay. From the air the plain was a magnificent sight, peppered as it was with the glittering testaments and offerings of generations of Buddhists, Noblemen and Kings. The building of such monuments was a supposed shortcut to Nirvana - "Oh great builder of pagodas" was a common greeting in Burma when assistance was required-and Pras had sworn to visit it on the ground just as soon as the war was over, assuming he hadn't already started his own journey in the builders' footsteps. Now, however, it was less of a shortcut than a signpost to where Pras hoped to delay the journeys of some other individuals. As he drew closer the blue haze of distance started to clear and he realised that this particular journey had, for some people, plainly begun. Above the plain a flight of Japanese fighters were wheeling and diving like vultures above the carcass of a stricken buffalo. He could just make out smoke coming from the ground and concluded that the convoy, or one following it, had been caught in the open, and was, as he watched, being strafed and bombed. He thought of the women, the children, the nurses and doctors, and of Jerry Osbourne. He wondered whether he would see or hear from him again. Images of violence fluttered through his head like moths as he watched the raptors continue their work, before banking violently and dropping altitude, hoping that they were too intent on their most easy of targets to notice him as he headed home. There was no way to get to Nyaung U now, his route was blocked, and his plane was slow and unarmed. If they spotted him, he was dead. If Jerry was waiting he'd have to wait some more, would probably have to walk out, the airspace was getting a little too hot for Pras to be gadding about in. And if he wasn't waiting? Pras felt sure they would both meet again eventually.

Pras took one look over his shoulder and muttered a silent prayer as he sped away. He said it for himself, as he knew that whoever was on the ground was beyond its reach.

2

We had begun the destruction of the oilfields on the fourteenth-the day that Magwe was overrun-after receiving the order to 'Deny and Evacuate'. We used sledgehammers and acetylene torches, dropping scrap iron down the wells and making firebombs we could use to destroy the tanks by filling bottles with oil, sealing them with wax and topping them up with acid. We prepared the power station by surrounding each of the four machines we had switched off with thirty-five pounds of gun cotton and were about to flood the buildings with oil when we were ordered to leave the plant ready to start up again. We shielded the seventy pound charge on the fifth machine, which we had kept running, with an asbestos sheet to prevent the heat from detonating it and I returned to the battery room to throw the switch, leaving the entire plant in a state of suspended desolation. The long walk along the switch gallery after I had set the batteries ready for their ultimate destruction was faintly disturbing, as I could see the line of machines, all set with their charges, the only noise the faint hiss of escaping steam from the last active boiler and the gentle cooing of a lone pigeon.

The last structure to be destroyed was, for me, the most upsetting. It was a somewhat Heath Robinson plant I had made in order to extract gasoline from the crude we had in abundance. It was, at least, gratifying that these stores were greatly appreciated by the beleaguered army units that were by now rolling through the town. As we set light to the fields the burning oil sent great globular clouds of thick, black smoke into the sky and before the day was out the Japanese had bombed the field manager's bungalow. We assumed this was merely to show their displeasure at our work as it had no possible military significance. The power station and outbuildings now prepared for destruction, we waited for the final order.

On the evening of the fourteenth we all ate what was to be our final club dinner, of roast jungle fowl and pigeon accompanied by aubergines, potatoes and tomatoes, all salvaged from the bungalows' well-tended gardens, and the remains of the club cellar. After dinner McAlistair, Briggs and Watson decided, in their somewhat inebriated state, to pack all their remaining silver into tin boxes and bury them in a pit recently dug by McAlistair's son, who had been evacuated with the rest of the women and children. It was a dark night, the moon obscured by the smoke from the burning fields, and they were anything but quiet as they transferred their valuables by bicycle, along with little bits and pieces from those of us who remained, and went about their business. I doubt the silver stayed there for long, as it was buried in full view of the servant's compound. The next morning I made my final trip to bungalow 86, my bungalow, which looked especially splendid in the clear morning light as it had only recently been painted. The gardens were still in magnificent order, the flower beds almost military in their precision, a well-organised riot of blazing colour, the winding bushes on the trellis had recently come into flower, and the fragrance of frangipani and vanilla filled the air. It was an oasis of calm in an increasingly mad world. Built of brick, unlike the servant's quarters, it resembled a Portuguese villa with its white stucco, its verandas and pillars and shutters. I didn't take anything, I knew I wouldn't have the room, I just wanted to see it one last time before we left. I knew I would never see it again, and I wanted all the memories it contained to stay with me. We then finished the demolition. It was deeply affecting to see so many years of hard work go up in smoke.

At noon we gathered near one of the bungalows for food and orders. We were all ready and standing by our forty or so cars, chrome glinting in the sunlight, perfect camouflage, when a certain Captain Jamieson of the Gloucestershire regiment passed me by. The Gloucestershires were one of the forces charged with the defence of Yenangyaung and the Captain stopped as he saw my Ford V8 saloon, my Minx had proved somewhat unsuitable for Burma's unmetalled roads, with myself and Gillespie sitting on the bonnet eating the sandwiches made up after a final raid on the remains of the club's larder. Looking us both up and down in that faintly superior way officers so often have with civilians, he made the comment that it looked 'more like bloody Ascot' than an evacuation. I decided to offer him the use of my car, as I certainly would not be getting out of Burma with it, and he readily accepted. Plainly he felt that Ascot was the kind of place he belonged, not us. Gillespie and I then filled up the back with various stores from the medical truck and our own larders before hopping into the space cleared in the back of the truck and starting the journey to Chauk. We received no word of thanks.

As the engines of the convoy started up with a noise like

the grunting of a herd of irritated elephants, a lone Japanese bomber flew almost sedately towards us, swooping low over the massed ranks of cars, causing their occupants to duck and dive out of doors and over tailgates, making for any available cover. Amazingly, he failed to drop any bombs, or even use his machine guns. We all watched in stunned silence, men half-way down ditches and cowering under the few trucks were frozen rigid and open-mouthed as the bomber disappeared into the distance almost as languidly as he had arrived. I can only presume that he was as amused as the Captain to see this long line of gentlemen in their cars troop slowly out of the town. Maybe he had forgotten that there was a war on.

About thirty miles from Yenangyaung, just before we headed West to Chauk, we were surprised to realise that the rare overcast sky, the cover of which we had been so grateful as we abandoned our homes, was in fact the smoke from the oilfields we had destroyed. It was only then that we understood just how serious our situation was, and how much of our life's work was now charred and blackened.

The road to Chauk was, luckily, well-gravelled and well-maintained, and as we drove through the parched and rolling hillsides we became more and more apprehensive. The skies, already ominously dark as a result of our work, were strangely quiet, and any moment we expected the whine of the Japanese planes alerted by the lone bomber as they swooped down onto us. They never came. Our journey was interrupted only once. The Pin Chaung was a fast-flowing river with a sandy bottom. If you stopped while fording it, your car would sink to its axles and have to be manhandled out. There was what seemed to be a permanent gang of Burmese who waited there just in order to profit from any extractions that were necessary. Only one of our

97

cars became bogged down, however, and we spent a nervy half hour dragging it out ourselves, much to the natives' chagrin. They felt that they had extraction rights, and an unpleasant scene was only avoided through more judicious re-distribution of the stores in our truck. We realised how lucky we were that the Monsoon had not seen fit to come early, for the river would then have become an impassable torrent, necessitating a lengthy and, given the circumstances, highly dangerous, diversion.

We arrived at Chauk late in the evening, ate and spent the night on various floors. The next day the majority of the convoy were sent along the river to Yenangyat, where Watson died of heat-stroke, while myself, Gillespie, McAlistair and a few others who were adjudged to know the area well enough stayed on and began the destruction of the oilfields around Chauk. Luckily these fields were smaller and presented less of a problem, and by the sixteenth we had finished, and had merely to finish dismantling the boilers and take any essential parts to be dumped in the river. We heard that the Japanese had been reported in Yenangyaung at six pm. We had left at two. This was one of a number of close shaves.

We stayed the night of the eighteenth on the SS Webbo which was one of the launches we were to leave on the following day. I, for one, failed to sleep at all.

3

'Where in blazes are we?' Captain Jamieson was getting fraught. Since the convoy of civilians had left Yenangyaung the town had been under attack almost constantly. After two days of hard combat the Japanese had been temporarily halted, though at great cost, and rumours of a new force spotted at Kyaukpadaung had led to the Captain, along with some assorted stragglers and the wounded, to be sent to Gwegyo in order to provide the troops being sent there with some local knowledge. The Japanese had not only advanced on Yenangyaung in great numbers in an attempt to capture the oilfields; some had used the dry bed of the Paunggwe Chaung, a southern tributary of the Pin Chaung, to approach the ford unnoticed, and had ambushed their column after an air attack had turned their tank escort into a blazing roadblock. The Captain had abandoned his car, a Ford V8 saloon he boasted about being given by a grateful fellow Etonian, and, along with five other men, run for cover into the scrub jungle where they were separated from the main force by the following ground attack.

'No idea, Sir.' Corporal "Chalky" White, a large, bluff Londoner, was thirsty. They were all thirsty. During the previous few days fighting lack of supplies had reduced them to drinking water from the radiators of abandoned vehicles, siphoning out the dirty, rust-stained liquid with pieces of piping ripped from the engines. It was ironic, thought Chalky, the town was swimming with fuel, but the water tanks had been destroyed by the Japanese almost immediately. He had seen the rest of his unit either killed or injured, and had been glad to be ordered North to act as a guide, though his credentials were less than impressive; he had been in Burma for just six weeks. The six men, unable to use the usual ford due to the Japanese advance, had crossed the Pin Chaung two miles or so downstream. They were lost. The previous night had been sticky and unpleasant, and they were all tired. 'I think we should still be heading West, Sir.'

'Is that for Chauk or Kyaukpadaung?'

'Chauk, Sir. We crossed downstream, so we should be nearer Chauk than Kyauk, Sir.' Chalky looked at his map, which was less of a map than a scribbling on the back of the military equivalent of a beer mat. This lack of basic supplies had made the campaign even more difficult than it should have been. 'That's right, Sir. Maybe Northwest would be better. Or we could head for the Irrawaddy, Sir, and follow it to Chauk.' Chalky looked despondently at the four men sprawled under the spreading shade of a Peepul tree. 'Lofty, you got any water left?' Private Richardson, predictably the tallest of the group, shook his head slowly and dolefully.

'Corporal,' the Captain was using his field glasses, 'there seems to be a hut up ahead. We'll ask. Father always said that a gentlemen never asks directions, but I'm afraid I'm going to have to disappoint him. Diseases desperate grown, and all that.' He started to stride away, the four men got to their feet slowly, and wearily, and the Corporal stared at them.

'Come on, lads, you how his nibs hates to be kept waiting.' In the short time they had known him, all five men had developed a healthy dislike for the Captain. He was in his late twenties, younger than Chalky by three years, and about the same age as three of the other four. Only "Bustie" Jacobs, a rather corpulent butcher's son, was appreciably younger, at twenty-three. Captain Jamieson treated them almost as servants, not even attempting to conceal his distaste for their accents, language or background. The Captain was born to lead, and he considered these men born to serve.

As Captain Jamieson strode purposefully into the distance, his men, weighed down with rifles and packs, struggled to keep up with him. They had walked for six or seven hours the previous day, in the burning heat of the Burmese hot season, and were exhausted. The only relief they had was in the fording of the river. The Captain had forbidden them to drink the water, for fear of disease, an order which Bustie and his principle tormentor, "Jock" Stevens had ignored. This was a mistake that would cost them both dear. Chalky turned to the men as they approached the solitary hut, perched on the edge of the rapidly approaching jungle.

'Can't be more than a couple of miles to go, lads.'

'Do what? We've been walking for bleedin' ever.'

'Exactly. It's the jungle. Look. It's getting thicker. Must mean there's water. Which means the river's getting near.' The men caught up with the Captain who had stopped about a hundred yards from the hut.

'Seems very quiet, Corporal. Take two of the men and scout around the back while I go in the front way.' He looked over at the bedraggled group of men he was forced to command. He felt a certain distaste at not being in charge of his old unit. They were smart, obedient. Jamieson had seen to that. They were also all dead. 'Jacobs. The Burmese respect girth, or so I'm told. A sign of wealth and all that. You come in with me.'

'Sir, I don't think you should go in, Sir. Too dangerous.'

'Nonsense, man. You take two men around the back, leave one here to cover the retreat and Jacobs and I will introduce ourselves. It's a Burmese hut. We're liberating them. Well, trying to. They wouldn't dare try anything. Off you go.' With that he strode towards the hut. Chalky took Richardson and "Sapper" Graham, a man too quiet and unassuming to warrant a more interesting nickname than his rank, leaving the increasingly pale-looking Jock at the side of the track. They skirted into the fringes of the jungle and worked their way slowly to the back of the hut. They didn't see the Captain and Jacobs walk straight in.

'Doesn't he bloody realise that for some of them, the Japanese are liberating them from us?' He stood still. 'Lofty, what do you make of that?' He pointed to the back of the hut where they saw the prostrate body of a native. His head lolled suspiciously to the side and he had flies buzzing around a wound in his chest. 'Bleedin' hell, let's get in there.' As soon as they started to move, they heard a pair of shots. The three men stood still, frozen with fear. In the silence that followed, Chalky waved Lofty round to the right of the hut, Sapper to the left, while he approached from behind. When they were all in position he counted to three with his fingers and they rushed simultaneously.

Lofty and Sapper took the front door, while Chalky flew through the flimsy rush mats which took the place of windows at the shape which he saw on the other side. He barrelled straight into a Japanese soldier who was aiming his rifle at the prostrate and bleeding form of Jacobs. The second Japanese soldier was kneeling on the ground beside him, searching his pockets. Chalky hit the floor and looked up, only to see the face of the second soldier disappear in an explosive haze of blood just as he brought his pistol to bear on him. Lofty stood impassively at the door, his rifle smoking as the man Chalky had jumped on was felled permanently with the butt of Sapper's Lee Enfield. It was over in seconds.

'Jesus. Stupid bleeder.' Chalky had seen the body of the Captain, throat slit ear to ear, lying in the corner. 'Bustie must have almost drawn blood.' Sapper was beside him. 'How is he?' Sapper looked up at Chalky.

'Not too bad. A lucky escape, I'd say. He's losing a lot of blood, though.' He had been shot in the shoulder, but had come to just as his comrades entered. His rifle was by his side. One of the shots had been his.

'Got any water?' Chalky took a canteen from one of the dead Japanese.

'Here.' Having handed the canteen to Sapper to give the wounded Bustie a drink, Chalky walked over to the Captain's body, and took his field glasses, Webley pistol and identification, along with his cigarette case. Feeling in his breast pocket, he removed a sealed and blood-stained letter, which was addressed to a certain Helena Chatsworth. 'What do you reckon, guys? Think she wants his blood on the final letter?'

'I think she's well rid of him.'

'Don't speak ill of the dead. It's not his fault he was a pompous idiot.' He looked around the bare and dirty room. Sapper had almost finished patching up Bustie. 'Lofty, fetch Jock. We'd better get going.' Bustie retched. 'Jesus, not this as well. He told you not to drink the river water.' Chalky wasn't feeling too good himself. He put the letter in his pocket and walked out of the hut, just to get the stench of blood, sweat and cordite out of his nostrils. He lit one of the Captain's cigarettes. He saw Lofty staggering back, stooping in order to hold Jock upright, his long arm reaching around his back, and wondered what he was going to do now. He looked up into the sky, and saw that it was black. 'Sapper?' he called, 'Reckon that's cloud, or smoke?' Sapper walked out of the hut, staggering under the weight of his colleague.

'Smoke, corp.'

'They've got oil at Chauk, haven't they?'

'That's right.'

'There we are then, it's a sign. Pillar of smoke, and all that.' He smiled to himself. 'Find the burning oil, and Bob's your uncle.' He stood up. 'Let's go. Straighten up, men.' He laughed. Bustie vomited, Jock groaned. 'And we'd best be quick.'

They walked along the jungle's scrappy fringe for an hour before finding a path which seemed to lead directly towards the smoke. Another hour and the jungle started to close in. It had slowly changed from a gentle scrub with small, stunted trees and bushes, to a rich, thick wall of deep green, the sun's rays reduced to a faintly yellow light. Two of the men hacked away at the plants with their bayonets, while the other supported both the ill Jock and the injured and ill Bustie. They had long since lost sight of the columns of smoke and were now following their last compass bearing. The giant Peepuls with their chattering societies of green and imperial pigeons and invisibly clucking jungle fowl, the great lines of trees, stitched together randomly with vines and creepers so that they resembled a continuous Becher's Brook, and the occasional calls of animals frightened by the men's crashing, all passed them by un-noticed, without comment. The men were starting to worry.

'Let's take a break. I'm done in.' Chalky sank to the ground, leaning up against a tree. 'What I'd give for a brew. How's Bustie?'

'Bad. I don't know if he'll last much longer. He's lost a lot of blood and this bug he's got is dehydrating him badly. They've both got diarrhoea, too. We need to find a hospital soon.'

'Brilliant. There should be one just around the corner. If not I'll find a rozzer and ask, shall I? Any ideas?' Chalky looked around at the exhausted men.

'Let's fire off a few shots. We'll be able to hear if anyone is close, if we're quiet afterwards. Maybe that'll tell us where they are?'

'Might as well. Fire off three. Then we'll listen.

4

On the morning of the nineteenth I awoke early after a restless night. After breakfast there was a rumour, which seems ludicrous now, that our fervent demolition work had been a little premature. Whether someone thought the Japanese were going to be content staying where they were or what I have no idea, but this meant that we spent the next few hours attempting to repair some of the dámage we had inflicted on the previous day. We managed to get one of the machines in the powerhouse on the verge of working again when we took a welcome break for lunch. The fields were still on fire around the town, the smoke still pouring into the sky when, at about two in the afternoon, we sat down in the long club house. Due to the imminent evacuation, lunch was light, and we were just finishing the soup, a rather hurried concoction of whatever vegetables were still available, when we heard three gunshots. They sounded close, maybe a mile away at most, and the entire room fell silent. We had just recovered from the shock and returned to our soup when McAlistair walked into the room, his calm outward demeanour contrasting with our now knotted stomachs and his sweat-drenched appearance. "Gentlemen, there is no need to hurry but it is reported that the Japs have just entered the town and I suggest that we leave forthwith." There was another moment's silence before we all left the table with what would most accurately be described as indecent haste.

Much to our chagrin, Gillespie and myself were dispatched, rifles in hand, in order to return the boiler we had spent all morning repairing to its former emasculated state, while the rest of the men boarded their launches and scuttled off upstream. We accomplished our task, with jagged nerves and ears hyper-sensitive to the most innocent of noises, within the hour. Returning to our launch, we heard another volley of three shots. Though we tried to board slowly and calmly, I don't think we succeeded. We were, however, not the only men suffering from a bout of last-minute nerves. The captain of our vessel was a refugee from Hong Kong, who had been pressed into service with the flotilla company. Waiting for us to complete the demolition of the oilfields, he had completed his own, presumably sympathetic, demolition of beer bottles. He thus set off in completely the wrong direction. One would think that on a river this is rather difficult, as there is usually only a choice between two directions, but for some reason he felt that the way to Yenangyat was downstream. The launch itself was normally operated in the lower reaches of the river, so the crew were equally ignorant of our destination. It took us half and hour of swift downstream progress to persuade them all that we were heading straight for the Japanese lines. Once the error was realised, the launch was turned around post-haste, and we set off in pursuit of the rest of our group.

Neither Gillespie nor myself were greatly confident of our arriving intact, as the water-level was low and the marking buoys had been removed, so progress was painfully slow. We should have been following the head launch of the group which had an experienced captain on board, but our diversion had isolated us. It was several hours before we both realised that our vigil at the bows, looking for, and sometimes feeling for with poles, the myriad sandbanks, was going to be compromised by our extreme tiredness. We therefore instructed two of the crew to take our places, and settled down for some sleep. The journey was likely to take another seven or eight hours, and it was already dark.

Having woken some time after dawn, both Gillespie and myself realised immediately that something was wrong. As we looked to the East we could see that we had overshot Yenangyat by some seven or eight miles. We were now gently chugging past Pagan. If we missed the rendezvous at Yenangyat, there would be no transport to get us through the Gangaw-Kelmyo-Tamu-Dimapur route. This was entirely the wrong place for us to be, as we knew many refugees would be trying the more northerly, and more difficult, routes of escape, such as through the Hawkaung valley, which was not for us an altogether enticing prospect. After a quick discussion we leapt into action, trying to persuade the captain to turn around and head back for Yenangyat while we still had the chance. He, however, was having none of it. It took a great deal of courage for us to do what we did next, as we were outnumbered and not exactly fighting men; we picked up the rifles we had been issued with for the demolition and pointed them at the captain, insisting that he turn the launch around. He relented.

At that point, our worries should have been over. A short trip downstream to Yenangyat, and then four hundred miles by car and lorry to India, and relative safety. We had, however, reckoned without the captain's inexperience, and, possibly, failed to take into account his probable hangover. The commotion had drawn the crew away from their task of watching out for sandbanks, so, with a sickening shudder, the launch duly found one of its own accord and ground to a halt.

There was an even greater commotion, and it was plain that the five man crew, along with us, simply did not possess the wherewithal to free the launch, even if we could agree on that as the best course of action. The crew and captain blamed us to a man, and one by one they all waded to the shore, which

107

happily was close. We were, unfortunately, on the East side of the Irrawaddy. If we had alighted on the West side, we could still have walked, but there was no way to cross for us now, so we followed the crew to the shore before sitting down on the river bank for a smoke in order to decide what our next move should be. It was at this point that the crew seemed to vanish, and we were left alone, with only our packs, each containing meagre rations and a water bottle, and two rifles. We both knew the area reasonably well, and agreed that we should head for the main road through Pagan, as we were bound to meet some convoy or other there.

We had walked for about half an hour when we found the convoy. Some of the vehicles were still smouldering from what appeared to have been a comprehensive air attack, presumably the day before. We searched through the vehicles, most of which were marked as belonging to the Red Cross, but could find no-one alive. There were bodies everywhere. We saw women, children, young and old. All were dead, and already there were carrion eaters at the scene, which flew off as we shooed them away, only to settle again as we walked onwards. I felt sick, but still kept my rifle held out in front of me, as if I expected one of the victims to suddenly leap forth from the remains of their vehicle and attack me. For some reason I felt partly responsible for all of this, after all, if we hadn't been in Burma, the Japanese would have seen no reason to invade, and if they had, would not have encountered any resistance. Now, certainly, there were factions within the native Burmans who were glad of the Japanese intervention, and were assisting them at every turn, or so I had heard.

Hanging backwards out of one truck, arms stretched outwards, was the body of a man in his mid-thirties. He had obviously got stuck halfway out of the window, though why he hadn't opened the door was beyond me, I supposed that as the truck was old, and quite battered, it was entirely possible that the door simply wouldn't open. Around his neck there was a camera, dangling from the strap which had twisted itself into knots and was gently swaying in the breeze. The man had several bullet-wounds to the chest, and looked strangely familiar. I walked up to his body slowly, and looked closely at his face. There was dried and caked blood running from his nose down his forehead and into his close-cropped, dirty blond hair, and his eyes were wide open, staring vacantly at me. I couldn't quite place him. A quick glance into the truck left me struggling to extricate some tubes which I assumed contained film, and I also took the unfinished roll from the camera. If he was a journalist, I thought that they might contain some useful photographs, possibly some firm evidence of the offhand way in which the Japanese treated civilians.

Gillespie and I felt vaguely ghoulish as we looked through the trucks and cars, primarily for water but also for food. We both wanted to bury the bodies but there were almost sixty, and but two of us. We knew we had to do whatever we could to escape. As we approached the head of the convoy we saw an old Wolsey, just sitting there, completely unscathed. We both knew that this was, if not the ticket out of there, at least one of our immediate problems solved. When we finally drew level we found a young girl, of about fourteen or fifteen, sitting in the back seat. She looked at us in surprise as we approached, asking us where Tinh was. We were too embarrassed to tell her that he was, without doubt, dead, and so proceeded to salvage as much petrol, water and food as we could, and checked the car over.

As we readied ourselves for departure, she sat stock still in the back seat, in complete silence, ignoring us completely. Even as we started the car up and drove away, making as wide a berth as we could around the vehicles and bodies in front of us, she said nothing.

5

Johannah Stewart crouched down at the edge of the jungle behind a stunted mango bush and watched in silent horror as the Japanese planes swooped and dived, unleashing blazing torrents of machine-gun fire onto the convoy of which she had, until recently, been a member. They seemed to her to be almost trying to land, they were so low, flying not more than fifty feet above the ground. The convoy had stopped on the road near Pagan village due to one of the leading vehicles sustaining a puncture, at which Johannah, along with several others, had rushed into the jungle for a much needed toilet break.

At school, Hannah, as her friends generally called her, was renowned as a slowcoach. Whenever there was something to do, or somewhere to go, she was always the girl who held everyone else up. The rest of the girls would form the regulation crocodile, each pair holding hands, and wait. As she sauntered into the yard, the nuns would be furious with her, shouting at her to hurry, but she would do no such thing. As far as she was concerned, someone had to be last, and seeing as she could never be first, her sister invariably taking this honour, academically as well as temporally, Hannah had decided that it should be her. Though a naturally gifted dawdler, she had also developed the unconscious skill of knowing exactly when to make her eventual entrance; as far as she was concerned, the best entrances were the ones accompanied by the most noise, and with the greatest possible number of eyes trained upon them. She was late again.

She hadn't decided to be the last back from the jungle, it was simply that she wasn't scared of the snakes and spiders and centipedes, some of which were poisonous, and all of which, to the other girls, were ugly beyond belief. She had discovered a particularly interesting spot, full of seething and twisting insect life, near the tree beside which she had chosen to relieve her aching bladder while prodding the ground with a stick to ensure she didn't choose an ant's nest or, even worse, a bee's nest upon which to pee. She had finally been pulled rudely from her voyeuristic reverie by the sound of approaching planes. This in itself was not a bad thing, as already Allied planes were rumoured to be dropping supplies to refugee convoys, and seeing as theirs was a Red Cross convoy, they didn't expect to be attacked by the Japanese. They were wrong. Within seconds the road and the fifty or sixty yards on either side before the jungle started became a killing field. Great vertical fountains of dust were kicked up by the impact of the bullets and bombs destroyed two or three of the trucks on the planes' first pass. She arrived on the edge of the jungle just as the planes finished their attack, and stared open-mouthed at the smoke and carnage in front of her. People were running about aimlessly and panicked like the chicken she had seen the family's servant decapitate one day before supper, and the air was rent with the screams of the injured and a sudden explosion from one of the trucks. It had been carrying ammunition.

The war had started for Hannah just before Christmas. She had returned from a holiday with friends near Mandalay, primarily a reward for her achievements at school that year, and was looking forward to yet more rewards come Christmas morning. What she received instead was a piece of shrapnel, about one inch long and one quarter of an inch round, in her left thigh. Though she knew the news from Singapore had been bad, she didn't truly think the war was real until that day, Christmas Eve 1941.

As her mother was working for the war effort, at a newly installed telephone exchange, she hadn't been evacuated along with the rest of the children. She stayed and ran errands for the Gurkha battalion which had been installed as guards. Her life had been running smoothly and enjoyably until one day, near the end of February, the general evacuation of Rangoon was ordered. She had enjoyed the excitement of sleeping all over the town, sometimes out of doors, and of being flirted with by all the soldiers. Now that was over. There was panic. The officers ran around threatening people with their pistols, saying they would shoot anyone who didn't leave immediately, and once she even saw them carry out their threats on some looters outside a department store. That was the first time she had seen a dead body. It was not to be the last. Her mother had panicked and sent her off with one of the diplomatic missions that was leaving; this was arranged by a friend of hers who was the son of the Chinese ambassador. She told Hannah to wait for her at Pyay, around one hundred and thirty miles North of Rangoon.

She had waited for a week, but her mother had failed to show up. Eventually she was virtually forced to join the Red Cross convoy which was heading North by a good-looking American journalist who had cajoled and flattered her, using up an entire roll of film taking photographs of her, and bribed her with Hershey bars before finally threatening physically to tie her up and put her in a truck if she refused to come willingly.

112

This convoy had proceeded to wind its way North in a torturously slow fashion, sometimes covering no more than fifteen or twenty miles in a day. They were plagued by mechanical failures, damaged bridges and difficult ford crossings which invariably captured one or more vehicles for an hour or two. They were sent the wrong way by natives, and got lost of their own volition on a number of occasions. Nevertheless, they were still almost a hundred miles ahead of the Japanese, whose advance had apparently slowed considerably in the past week. The journalist seemed to disappear and reappear with astonishing regularity; he had only rejoined them three days before, after an absence of almost a week.

Now she watched dumbfounded as the men and women rushed around, attempting to minister to the wounded and get back into the trucks and cars that were undamaged. She stood up to run back to the car she was travelling in, a battered old Wolsey, when she heard the whine of the Japanese planes once more. She threw herself to the ground and covered her ears as the rattling of the machine guns and the low thud of the bombs which were followed by the explosions which seemed to rip the still air apart. For ten minutes the planes bombed and strafed the convoy until they disappeared as suddenly as they had arrived, and there was silence once more. This time there were no screams.

She ran through the jungle for what seemed like hours before seeing a building which was only a mile or so from the village they had just passed. It was getting dark so she walked in, grabbed the first person she came across and asked if she could stay for the night. The Burman gave her a bowl of thin soup and showed her to the landing, where she lay down and slept fitfully, all the time wondering where her mother was. During the night she was continually woken by the noise of people walking up and down the corridor, in and out of the many doors which led off it and a constant, low murmuring. At four in the morning she realised what the building was, and left.

Hannah sat alone on a fallen tree at the edge of the jungle, thinking. In the space of two months she had lost her home, her mother, at least as far as she knew, and now the few belongings she had brought with her were almost certainly destroyed. She resolved to return to the car and see what she could salvage before continuing on foot. She followed the road away from the village and, after half an hour, saw the first vehicle; the truck which had been bringing up the rear. It was a charred and skeletal wreck, but nevertheless still smouldering, and she stopped in the middle of the track. She was always the last. And she was caught between wishing she wasn't, so that she had died along with the rest of the convoy, and being glad that she was so easily distracted. It was all that had stood between her and certain death. It struck her as amusing that the very thing that her mother and her teachers and her friends insisted would cause her to come to no good was the very thing which had saved her life. She resolved to continue, if only so as not to disgrace her mother, who would certainly have had something to say had she given up. She started to walk again.

She walked past the twisted bodies of people who, over the past few weeks, had become friends. She saw Penny Davis, a half-Burmese girl who had been travelling with her six-month old brother, Matthew. He was clutched in her arms, wrapped in a blanket, as if she was still trying to protect him. She passed the body of Mrs Jenkins, who had been kind enough to give her some clothes when she joined the convoy in Pyay. She stopped as she saw the body of the American hanging out of the window of one of the trucks. Then she turned away, she couldn't bear to look any more.

When she arrived at the Wolsey, it was empty. It was also undamaged. She thought that maybe Tinh, the Vietnamese driver, was also unhurt, as she hadn't seen his body. She opened the door, drank some water from the canteen on the front seat, and sat down quietly in the back.

She had been sitting absolutely still, just as Sister Agnes always wished she would, for over an hour when she sensed that someone was approaching the car.

6

We had been driving for about an hour before she spoke. The road was gradually getting worse, and had degenerated into barely more then a dirt track. As we moved forward the surface was thrown up into a thick, choking cloud of dust which broke away from the front of the car like water. It not only covered every exposed part of the body but crept perniciously down boots and underneath clothing where, once established, it seemed to seep into the very pores of the skin. It soon felt as if we were as filthy inside as we plainly were outside. As Gillespie drove, I improvised some face-masks out of one of the girl's skirts, and soon we were barrelling along like three highwaymen, resplendent in our flowery face protectors. I had looked into the back seat to check that the girl was all right, and noticed that she looked in pain. I asked if she needed to go to the toilet but she shook her head so vigorously and instantaneously I knew she had to be lying. I told Gillespie to stop the car. She looked scared and I asked what the matter was. All she would say is that we had to go with her. I looked at Gillespie and he looked at me, both of us confused, but she was adamant, so we relented.

We walked through the scrub towards a Peepul tree and relieved ourselves against it while the girl crouched behind a bush, far enough away to preserve her modesty but not so far away that she didn't have us in sight the entire time. We were both terribly embarrassed. As she crouched down she seemed to be nervously scanning the sky, before looking as if to check we were still there, and then, satisfied that we were, turning her gaze onto the heavens once more. We could see she was scared but had no idea of what, it certainly didn't seem to be us, and she didn't seem to want to let us in on the secret. We lead her back to the road, where we all jumped into the car, pulled on our masks, and drove off.

A quick glance at our map and the sure knowledge that the Japanese would be advancing steadily lead Gillespie and myself to agree that the best course of action would be to stick to the Irrawaddy as closely as possible, to avoid the chances of running into them. If we took the usual route to Mandalay we would have cut back Eastwards in order to get onto the good roads. This seemed a little too dangerous, as well as, we thought, increasing our chances of being caught in the open by the Japanese air force. It meant we had to continue to use the unbelievably dusty roads we had travelled on thus far, but as we expected to be in Mandalay long before the rains rendered them impassable, we felt it was worth the risk. We planned to reach Myingyan by nightfall, and see if there were any boats nearby – the Pagan to Mandalay boat would usually stop there – and if not, carry on driving for the remaining the forty or fifty miles the next day.

Our plans went a little awry, as only five miles or so from Myingyan the Wolsey ground to a shuddering halt. We were all hot, tired and filthy from the trip, which had taken far longer than we had expected due to the condition of the roads, and it was already getting dark. We pushed the car off the track and decided that, before Gillespie and I fixed it – we were, after all, engineers – we should eat. The girl watched, reticent as ever, while we made a fire and started to boil some water. Neither Gillespie or I were experienced cooks, there was the club or our wives for that sort of thing, so we filled the pot full of water to the brim with rice before rigging up a light from the car battery to work by. The girl, whose name, we had discovered, was Hannah, sat under a tree watching us closely as we attempted to discover the cause of the breakdown. The way that the car had suddenly ground to a halt suggested a lack of fuel, but there should have been plenty left in the tank, a suspicion soon confirmed as Gillespie crawled underneath to check for holes. There were none, and the tank was still over half full. I took a quick look at the carburettor and discovered our problem immediately; it, along with the fuel lines, was clogged with dust. I stared at it, realising I would have to dismantle the entire assembly in order to clean it, a job which I imagined would take two or three hours, when suddenly we heard a slight voice admonish us.

'You men really are useless.' It was Hannah. We turned around to see her spooning great piles of rice into bowls; we had somewhat over-estimated the amount necessary for the three of us. After she had filled two bowls with the half-cooked and somewhat inflated rice, she turned to us both. 'You get on with the car. I'll cook.' We were struck dumb, partially from embarrassment, partially from surprise at hearing the girl speak

117

without being forced to. We watched as she rooted in one of the packs, pulling out a tin of bully beef, which she opened and sliced before placing onto another pan she had liberated. We went back to the rather sorry-looking engine and started the job of stripping it. 'Supper's ready.'

We dined heartily on what I imagine could be called a risotto of bully beef and tinned tomatoes. Then she cleaned our plates as we returned to our task. When we had finished, some three or four hours later, she was fast asleep, curled up in the back seat, covered by an old army blanket she had taken from one of our packs. We didn't have the heart to test the engine and wake her, so we had a cigarette and slept by the side of the car, rifles over our laps. We woke up to find tea already brewing. The car started first time.

It wasn't long before we reached Myingyan, but were immediately struck by the seemingly hostile nature of the natives. As we had heard that some were assisting the Japanese, we were very wary as we drove into the village. Gillespie spoke an amount of Burmese, and on production of a tin of bully beef was able to question one of the more friendly-looking residents, and was told that not only were no boats expected, but also a rumour that the Japanese had occupied Kyaukpadaung. It didn't take long to decide that waiting was maybe not our best option, so we re-filled our water bottles from the village well and went on our way, giving some spare food to a few of the villagers in the hope that they would not be quite so hostile to any other refugees who passed through.

After leaving the village, Hannah started to say that she wanted to go to Sagaing, where she apparently had relatives. We told her we would go to Mandalay, and see what the situation was before making a decision. She protested for a few miles but eventually lost heart and proceeded to sulk all the way to Mandalay. The journey was slow but uneventful. The closer we got to Mandalay, the more the roads became clogged with refugees, mainly on foot, walking beside bullock carts laden with what seemed to be their entire worldly goods. On the outskirts of Mandalay we met some British soldiers who advised us that our best option was to head straight for the river where a number of boats were readying to leave for Katha and Bhamo, in order to help the refugees get to Myitkyina where the evacuation was being carried out by air. Gillespie and I made an executive decision. Hannah would be better off with us than wondering around on her own in order to find some relatives who had doubtless already packed their bags and left. This decision did little to improve her mood.

Mandalay was packed with people, all desperate to get on the next boat out. We had to abandon the Wolsey, which saddened me, as it was a fine car, breakdowns notwithstanding, and it seemed a pity to leave it to its fate. We loaded up our packs with everything which we thought could be of use, as much food as we could carry, and cigarettes and some whisky in case we needed to bribe anyone.

The war had started to affect me, and Gillespie. We both thought things we never would have in peacetime. We took our rifles. They were very useful in getting crowds to part before us. We had no uniforms, but we were plainly important British men, as we had rifles, and our dust-caked and filthy appearance didn't stop us receiving more than our fair share of respect when dealing with the army. We pushed, prodded and fought our way to the foreshore, where we met an acquaintance of Gillespie's, a supercargo called Jeffreys. He told us he was to leave on a hospital ship on Monday morning, it was now late on Saturday, and we should stick close by if we wanted to accompany him. He assured us they would be glad of the extra hands, especially engineers, as the foreshore had been heavily bombed the previous morning, and several of their boiler inspectors and engineers had been either killed or badly wounded. We readily agreed.

We spent the night a few hundred yards from the boat, called the Assam, in a textile factory. It was the most comfortable night I could remember. What seemed like weeks of sleeping rough and on people's floors was immediately forgotten as the three of us rolled up yards upon yards of cloth to make a soft, comfortable mattress. Hannah still clutched the blanket she had appropriated from us.

The next morning we went to the Assam. The sight that greeted us almost made us want to walk to Bhamo.

7

"Chalky" White lay gently back, letting the front wheel of the jeep take his entire weight as he handed Lofty a cigarette from the deceased Captain's case. Sapper was tending to their sick comrades. They were both hospitalised in the makeshift sick bay which had been installed in the old clubhouse as soon as five men had staggered out of the jungle. A short time after letting off their three shots, the men had heard a series of explosions. They hadn't sounded like artillery, so, taking a bearing on the sound, they loosed off another three shots in order to alert whoever was there to their imminent arrival, and set off. After another four hours of hacking through the jungle, they walked into the outskirts of Chauk. They had travelled a little over three-quarters of a mile. They had been greeted by a regular army unit which had plainly just arrived. Now, however, they were wondering what they were going to do next.

'Corporal?'

'Yes, Sir?' Chalky looked up to see the unit's Sergeant Major staring down at him.

'Sar'nt Major to you, Corporal. I trust that silver cigarette case was about to be returned, as it is presumably the property of the deceased Captain?'

'Yes Sar'nt Major.' He fished in his pocket to retrieve the offending item. 'There you are, Sar'nt Major.' He also took the blood-stained letter and placed both articles in the man's palm.

'Thank you, Corporal.' He removed the cigarettes and held them out in his hand. 'I think you may keep these, Corporal.'

'Thank you, Sar'nt Major.' Chalky sheepishly took the cigarettes from the outstretched hand. He knew the penalties for looting the dead, and if this man hadn't once been an mere infantryman himself, he felt sure he would now be forming a more intimate acquaintance with them.

'You did a good job, Corporal. I suggest that after you've rested, you hop into a jeep and head off to Kyaukpadaung, as was originally planned. The rest of your unit, what's left of it, has been sent to Myitkyina. That'll be your next stop, when you have finished at Kyauk. Let's say that you leave at eighteen hundred hours. You'll be there by nightfall. Carry on, Corporal.' He turned on his heels and left.

'Another lucky escape, Corp.' Lofty had stopped attempting to hide his grin.

'We're full of them this week.' They both went a little quiet, then Sapper arrived, looking pale. Chalky looked up. 'How are they?'

121

'Not very good, Corp. Jock'll recover, he's only got dysentery, though there's a remote possibility he's contracted typhoid as well, apparently, but Bustie…' He hesitated. 'I don't think Bustie'll make it. He's got an infection in the wound. Pretty bad, by all accounts. The Doc said it would have been fine on its own, but what with the dysentery, and the time, and the heat, it doesn't look too good.' He sat down beside the other two men. 'What now?'

'We get two hours of R'n'R, and then a jeep to Kyaukpadaung. I suggest you get your head down.'

Three hours later they were in Kyaukpadaung. The rumours that the Japanese had penetrated this far were false, and plainly based on the fact that a large Chinese unit had arrived there some two days previously. After a short consultation with the Chinese commanding officer, who assured them that they were in no need of guides, it was decided that the three men should proceed to Myitkyina via Mandalay, following the rest of their unit, in order to assist with the evacuation of both civilians and the army wounded. Their driver returned to Chauk while they hitched a lift on a lorry full of Chinese wounded. Their journey took three days, during which seven of the Chinese soldiers died. None of them were buried; they were simply thrown out of the lorry.

The journey to Mandalay was uneventful, though the men were shocked not only at the apparent callousness of their allies' behaviour, but also at the massive increase in numbers of the refugees on the roads as they approached the city. It seemed as if the entire country was on the move, and they looked over the lorry's tailgate at the sorry-looking and weary travellers as they trundled past, trying not to catch their eyes, while simultaneously trying to ignore the people they saw falling by the wayside, exhausted. When they finally arrived at Mandalay they were greeted by a similar sight, except it was worse. The entire city was turning into a refugee camp, and was a far cry from the city of glittering temples that legends and Kipling described. It was now a squalid and overcrowded mess of begging children and dying adults and crime and filth and murder; it seemed that anything was acceptable when it came to escape.

The lorry made for the fort where the three men began to help ferry the wounded, of which the twenty or so survivors on their lorry were but a small addition to the hundreds simply lying about, waiting for evacuation, to the shore and thence to the waiting ship, the Japan. They had been ordered to take this ship as far as Katha, where it would have to stop as its draught was too great for the lower water level that far up-river. While they were ferrying men to and fro, a storm blew up, forcing the waiting ship to move into the middle of the stream, and half and hour later, it simply steamed off, regardless. Chalky and his men commandeered a lorry and drove overnight, as near to the river bank as they could, eventually catching and boarding the ship the next morning. They were on their way.

Five days later they arrived at Katha, where a rumour that the Japanese were not far away lead to the ship being scuttled as soon as most of the wounded had been transferred to shore. Chalky, Lofty and Sapper swam and waded through the water to the shore.

'Jesus, this is turning out to be a bit of a mess. What do we do now?' Sapper looked expectantly at his NCO, his dripping clothing steaming gently in the hot sun.

'I suppose we find out whether there are any trains running. Do you reckon we'll be able to sneak on without a ticket?'

Chalky laughed. 'Looks like that's where the wounded are being taken. I suppose we'd better lend a hand.'

'Can't we just, you know, wander off and get lost, Corp?'

'No we bloody well can't, Lofty. This is our job, and let's do it properly. You've seen what happens to these Chinese if they fall by the wayside, the least we can do is help them. After all, if it wasn't for them, the Japanese would probably be here by now.' They all walked off towards a stationary lorry, which was being slowly loaded with the non-walking wounded. For the next five hours they loaded men on, drove to the station, unloaded them, and returned to start the whole process again, while all the time refugees were gathering at the train station; this influx of wounded men suggested to them that a train would soon be here. They were right, and the moment the engine appeared, pulling about five carriages, the entire mass of people moved as one, pushing and shoving, trying to get a seat. It was plain to Chalky that only walking wounded would be able to get aboard, and even they would have trouble. The rest would have to wait for cattle-trucks and other flat-bed wagons suitable for the non-mobile, who were by far the majority. They climbed on board, in order to help people on, hoping at least to be able to police the boarding in order to avoid any more disasters.

'Corp, we're never going to able to stop this many people.'

'No, you're absolutely right. Let's just fill this carriage up, try to only let women, children and the wounded on, and then we'll shut the doors. Got that?' The other two men signalled that they had understood and took position inside each of the doors to the final carriage. They struggled to keep men who were not wounded off the train, resorting to violence more than once. As a boy, Chalky had been a tearaway, but the army had disciplined him and he was now the reigning regimental

124

heavyweight boxing champion, so it didn't take many incidents to persuade the able-bodied to seek their entrance elsewhere. In ten minutes, the train was full and started to pull slowly from the station, and as it did so, hundreds more men rushed at it out of the jungle, Chinese soldiers and refugees, clambering onto the top and hanging off the sides, Indian-style.

'You boys all right?' Chalky shouted down the packed carriage. He heard his comrades shout back.

'Thank you so much, young man. I don't know how we would have got out if it hadn't been for you.' Chalky turned to see a middle-aged woman with a young boy in her arms. 'I don't know who he is. I just grabbed him as we came to the train.' She smiled. 'Melissa Stewart, and you are?'

'Chalky, I mean, Corporal White, Ma'am.' He shifted uncomfortably. This woman was obviously from the Captain's class, yet she seemed to treat him as an equal. This was something he simply was not used to.

'When I get out of here I'll recommend you for a medal.'

'I'll settle for simply getting out of here, Ma'am.'

'Please, call be Melissa. And you are?' At that point, the whine of aircraft filled the air, and bright pin-pricks of daylight appeared in the train's skin as bullets suddenly ripped through it.

'Get down, under the seat.' He barked, and Melissa obeyed, after which he placed his body in the gap between the seat and the aisle, squeezing up as closely as he could. 'Sorry about this, Ma'am, I mean, Melissa.' He said in an embarrassed tone as the sound of machine-gun fire filled his ears. He looked up to see the shapes of men falling from the top of the train. He prayed. For the first time in his life.

8

As we boarded the Assam we reeled backwards in shock at the conditions. Gillespie and myself stopped at the end of the gang plank, wondering whether it wouldn't be more sensible to walk to Bhamo. In the end, I carried Hannah through the massed ranks of the wounded, trying to simultaneously cover her eyes and my mouth in order to prevent myself from vomiting. The decks were littered with wounded men, and the stench from their wounds, most of which already seemed to be gangrenous, was simply appalling. Jeffreys was waiting for us, an almost apologetic look on his face as we stepped over the bodies of what would soon, we suspected, be dead men. He told us that after the bombing, the chief engineer had no men under his command whatsoever, so we descended to the engine room and presented ourselves for duty. It was with a sense of overpowering relief that we found ourselves in the very bowels of the ship, wrapped in the thick and powerful odour of lubrication oil and charred wood. It was as if we had come home; oil was something we both understood, and its effect was not simply to cover the stench of the dying, but it also soothed our nerves and settled our stomachs. We decided that it would be better if Hannah was kept below decks, so we installed her, with our bags, in a utility room. Once, while our backs were turned, she sneaked away, presumably to explore. Neither Gillespie nor myself realised until we saw her standing at the top of the stairs on her return, wraith-like and ashen, a look of horror on her face.

The orders were for steam at zero seven-thirty hours. No-one in the engine room thought this was likely, but after Gillespie and myself seconded some of the fit Chinese soldiers and a motley crew of assorted natives, we were pretty close to achieving it, though with a slightly revised estimate, when a Chinese Colonel came aboard and requested that departure be delayed by another seven hours. Apparently the train carrying our next five hundred casualties had been delayed due to a crash near Htonbo. The story was that a troop train had been too heavily loaded to climb a hill, and so the Chinese had decided to uncouple half of it for later collection. Unfortunately, the rear half of the train had no brakes, so it immediately rolled back down the hill, hurtling straight into the following hospital train, killing twenty people. We appreciated the delay, as it gave us more time to prepare for the journey. When we finally left, the next morning, the boat was loaded with fifteen hundred men in various states of distress and quite a lot of equipment, none of which seemed to be anything other than military in nature.

As we looked back at Mandalay, we saw the first column of smoke, which was preceded by a number of explosions. Though gunfire had been reported nearby during the night, we presumed it was the demolition squad back on duty. Both Gillespie and myself felt a deep affinity with those poor men, ever destined to be the last out. We returned to our tasks with vigour, though I was starting to feel anything but well. Within a few hours, however, we had stopped again, as the Chinese had seemingly failed to bring any food aboard. Gillespie and I took the opportunity to take Hannah ashore, in order that all three of us could get some fresh air in our lungs. It was a mistake. On-board, we had become used to the stench of death and oil and burning wood, so that we hardly noticed it as we picked our way through the obstacle course of prostrate men on the deck. When we returned, an hour or so later, however, our lungs clear and our senses keen, the wall hit us again. If anything, it seemed worse than the first time. We had taken the chance to eat onshore, but only Gillespie held onto his lunch for any length of time, both Hannah and myself were violently sick within minutes of re-boarding the vessel. Though unpleasant at the time, this incident seemed to delay the onset of the dysentery I was later to suffer terribly from.

The next day passed slowly and without incident until we started to have trouble with the circulating pump. We requested that we put ashore in order to effect running repairs, and also to send parties out in order to look for fuel, which we were starting to run short of. We stopped at a small village, near to Singon, upon which the able-bodied Chinese poured across the gangways and proceeded to loot the village. We were unaware of this event as we were busy tracking down the leaking condenser which was the cause of our trouble, when Hannah ran in and asked us to come quickly. Alarmed, we sped to the deck and watched in horror as the entire village was systematically destroyed, to the point where even the houses were torn down. Both ourselves, Jeffreys and the Captain were complaining to the Chinese officers but either they simply didn't care, or they had no control over their men. As we raged and screamed, they simply shrugged their shoulders at us before walking ashore to direct the destruction. If there was one good thing to come out of that incident, it was that we were presented with forty-eight good stacks of fuel. Enough to see us to Bhamo.

The next day Gillespie passed out from exhaustion, and spent the rest of the voyage being lovingly cared for by Hannah. She had been upset because there was nothing for her to do, no way for her to help, especially as the Chinese were uncooperative and often familiar to the point of rudeness with her. The officers did nothing, and there were no Doctors. After two attempts to minister to the wounded, she retired, feelings hurt and strangely ashamed, to her room. Gillespie's illness, however, gave her a whole new lease of life; she had a purpose, and she stuck to her task like a trooper.

That night we anchored astern of the Japan, which we had caught up, and which carried a quantity of Burma Rifles as well as the almost ubiquitous wounded Chinese. We spent several nervy hours down below as the Captain talked to his opposite number. Apparently there were rumours regarding the Japanese, and the Japan was intending to go no further than Katha. The Captain agreed that a stop at Katha was the most sensible, and returned to tell the Chinese Colonel the new plan. It was at this point that the rumour spread about the crew that we should be ready to abandon ship with all due speed, and then we heard nothing. The Chinese officers were starting to prowl the lower decks armed with pistols, something they had not done previously. It was clear that they wished to proceed, and that they would object forcibly if we refused. The Captain then returned to the Japan, explained the situation and asked for assistance from the Burma Rifles should the Chinese object. By all accounts the reply he received indicated that the war was considered to be over for this particular battalion, and that we could expect no help whatsoever.

The decision was therefore made to continue to Bhamo, accepting the risk that the Japanese may already be there. We set off slightly before the Japan, and, after passing straight through Katha, saw the boat stop, disembark, and then shudder, an explosion splitting its hull. The remaining people on board simply swam ashore. The boat had been scuttled. This did not fill us with good cheer. An hour later, we were beset by another mechanical problem, though luckily there was no nearby village to suffer from our misfortune.

By this time, the mood amongst the few non-Chinese was very dark. The Chinese themselves were starting to get very jumpy, and there were several incidents between them which ended in gunshots. We were glad to be hidden below. Gillespie was starting to recover and Jeffreys paid a visit to inform us that, when we finally arrived at Bhamo, we were to be ready for immediate evacuation. The defile there was barely inches wider than the boat, and he wasn't at all sure that he could successfully guide us through. He said he would give us a warning, and after then we were to be ready to go as soon as the boat hit anything solid. Again, this failed to lift our mood greatly. We had been largely abandoned by our seconded Chinese crew, and those of us who remained at work were exhausted by our efforts to keep the craft going. The idea that we could have come all this way to simply run aground was not a happy one. It was then that the old fears, largely forgotten as we slaved away in our hermetically-sealed environment, of the Japanese air force re-surfaced. As it was, Jeffreys negotiated the defile like a man born to the task, and we anchored mid-stream.

We sat in the middle of the river for hours, while the Captain attempted to discover what he was to do. Three hours later, we moved alongside and again sat there, waiting. We were effectively crew now, and thus to stay with the Assam until it had received orders. It seemed strange to sit there waiting while the Chinese gradually removed their men from the boat. It was, however, a relief to see the back of them.

Later the same evening, a lorry turned up, and we were all urged to abandon ship and escape. In less than ten minutes we were off. The Captain had been away seeing the District Commissioner, apparently to negotiate passage to Myitkyina, possibly by plane. The news that the Japanese had crossed the

Shweli bridge and were moving swiftly to Bhamo in lorries had precipitated an almost immediate evacuation. It had, he said, taken much shouting and tearing of hair to get a lorry sent back to the Assam to collect us. We were on our way once more, to the District Commissioner's house, from where our journey would start, once more in convoy.

9

'Is it over?' Melissa whispered to Chalky as the entire train went quiet. The sound of the planes still buzzed in Chalky's ears as if his head was full of hornets, but he knew that they had gone, satisfied with their day's work. After the first few seconds of what was an almost supernatural calm, the moans and cries of the wounded began to start, gradually increasing as if the pain only really came when the threat of sudden death had passed.

'I think so, yes. They would have come back by now if they meant to. I reckon it was just an opportune attack. Probably on their way to somewhere far more interesting and didn't want to waste too many of their bullets on a mere trainful of refugees and Chinese.' He stood up, slowly, and walked to the window, stepping over the corpse of one of the other passengers who hadn't been quite so lucky. He looked out of the shattered window and saw that the area surrounding the track was littered with bodies. The train had ground to a halt as soon as the planes attacked, and now that they had gone, those external passengers who had run off for cover in the jungle were starting to filter back. Chalky saw Melissa get up. 'I wouldn't if I were you.'

'I'm sure I've seen much worse.' She said as she stood by his side. 'Good Lord. Hadn't we better try to get some of the wounded back on board?'

'I suppose so. Lofty.' He shouted. There was a guttural grunt in reply. 'Sapper.' Silence. 'Sapper?' Then he heard Lofty's voice echo through the carriage.

'I'm afraid not, Corp. War's over for Sapper.' Chalky stood stock still for a moment, contemplating how many of his friends he had already lost, before shouting back.

'Get his tags, water and anything else, then throw him out. Let's get all these bodies out, see if we can get some more wounded inside.' There was a moment's silence. 'Private Richardson, please obey orders.'

'Yes, Corp.' Chalky looked around him and saw that there were four casualties in his section. He lifted the first, a Burmese man of about sixty, on to his shoulders with a grunt and made his way to the door. He slipped on the final step and soldier and body hit the ground with a thud.

'You all right down there, Chalky?' It was Melissa, dragging the body of a sixteen year-old girl out of the carriage.

'Fine, thank you. Leave that to me, if you want to help, see if there's anyone out here who we can save.' He looked up and saw that the ex-roof dwellers were making their way back to the train. 'And you'd better hurry, or we'll not even get back on board.' Luckily the returning passengers remembered Chalky's exploits when they had first tried to board, and avoided the door of his carriage, simply climbing back onto the roof. He had just removed the final body on board and was going to pick up a casualty that Melissa had identified when the train started to strain and screech as the engine took up the slack. 'Melissa. Back onto the carriage, now.' She hopped back on as he lofted the Chinese man she had pointed him towards onto his shoulders and started to run alongside the carriage as the train started to move. He dumped the man through the door, there was no time to be delicate now, and then had to sprint as the train gathered speed. He hopped on at the last possible minute, grabbing the hand rail and swinging himself onboard, almost stepping on the wounded man as Melissa struggled in vain to drag him inside.

'That was close.' Having laid out the casualty on the floor in the aisle, he sat down, exhausted. 'Lofty?'

'Still here, Corp.'

'Better give me those tags.' He was about to take a drink when he remembered himself, and offered the canteen to the woman and boy.

'No, after you, it's not as if I've done any work.' She smiled. 'May I ask you something?'

'If you like.'

'Why Chalky?'

'Chalky White. We're not very adventurous with our nicknames in the army. I mean, look at Private Richardson.' He motioned towards the tall, lumbering character squeezing through the mass of people still inside and stepping gingerly over the injured as he walked down the carriageway towards them. 'Take one guess why we call him Lofty.' He laughed. 'We had a Bustie and a Jock, too, but they were left at Chauk. No prizes for guessing where they got those names, either. In fact, I was once in a unit that had no less than seven Jocks, three Busties and one other Chalky. Infantrymen are not renowned for their imagination. It must be hell serving in the Glamorgans.' They went silent. Both thinking about those who they had lost already, and trying not to think of who would be next. Then Chalky fell asleep.

Seven hours later, the train stopped with a shudder, rousing the sleeping Chalky, who looked across to see that Melissa had stopped trying to make the injured man he had rescued drink. 'What happened?'

'We've stopped.' Melissa replied.

'Why? Did you hear anything?'

'Nothing.'

'Lofty, take a look, will you?'

'Right you are.' The tall soldier leapt out of the carriage and stood, staring for a minute before jumping back in. 'Reckon we walk from now on. There's no steam coming from the engine, and the crew seem to be arguing amongst themselves. Oh, and there's been a skirmish here. A lot of dead bodies. A few days old, too, by the smell.' He sat down.

'How far to Myitkyina?'

'You don't want to know. We certainly can't take any wounded now, it's every man for himself.' Chalky looked at Melissa, who was cradling the injured man in her arms. 'Not unless you want us to carry him for the next sixty miles.' He looked at Lofty. 'We'd better get going. Collect everything you can. It's going to be a long trip. Four days minimum.'

They all grabbed whatever they could carry; food, water and blankets, and jumped out of the train. It was only then that they realised just how many people had been on board. The area around the train was buzzing with people, like the flies that buzzed over the corpses that were littered all around the clearing in which the train had stopped. There must have been two thousand people, all unsure what to do, where to go.

'Which way do we go?' Melissa was looking worried.

'Well, it seems that following the tracks will be our best option. We're bound to get there eventually.' They looked at each other in silence. 'The sooner we start, the better. The further we can get away from this place, the better.' They started to troop up the side of the train, and about this time, everybody else had the same idea. Soon there was a line almost a mile long of ragged refugees, walking along the railway track, hoping that the Japanese had better things to do than attack them.

Once the column was a few miles North of the train, and well away from the stench of decay which had followed them, only gradually growing weaker, dusk was already threatening to envelop them, and the huge mass of refugees ground to a halt with an almost telepathic will. Those amongst them that had failed to carry any water dug holes until it began to seep upwards, forming muddy pools from which they would drink greedily. There was an intangible feeling of relief in the air, as people slowly realised that they had escaped, and that they were, to all intents and purposes, free. No longer must they rely on others to aid them, now it was down to them, and there was a sense of camaraderie which had failed to appear before, when there had been a chance to gain the seat on the train, expel someone else from the carriage so that you may occupy it. The fact that the entire column was in exactly the same situation, and that there was no advantage to be had over others produced a tangible change of atmosphere.

'This column almost feels happy, don't you think, Chalky?' Melissa was sitting down, her back propped up against a tree, cradling the head of the child she had rescued in her lap.

'You just wait until everyone starts to get hungry, and thirsty. Watch all this goodwill evaporate then. This is simply that period of joy you feel after surviving something you didn't expect to survive. It'll pass, mark my words. It always does.' Chalky was suspicious, as he always was of periods of calm.

'You are such a cynic. Have some faith.'

'Oh, I had faith. Once. So did Sapper. And Charlie, and

Bustie, too, I shouldn't wonder, and dozens of others I could name. It didn't get them very far, now did it?' He pulled one of the last cigarettes out of his pocket and lit it, drawing deeply on the smoke, knowing it would be one of the last he would have for a while, if not at all. 'We felt like this after the first attack at Yenangyaung.'

'You were at Yenangyaung?'

'Yes, why?'

'I used to live there. How was it?'

'Pretty unpleasant. There weren't that many of us at first, and we had no tank support. Luckily the Japs can be a little gung-ho, and we only lost three men in the first attack. This was exactly what our position felt like. Calm. Elated, even. Then they attacked again, and again, and again. By the time we were relieved, only five of us were walking. We had been seventy-two. Since then, one's gone down with dysentery, possibly typhoid, one's dead and one's almost certainly dead. Two men walking. Seventy-two into two. And this just in the past week.' He fell silent, and passed the remains of his cigarette to Lofty. 'And you wonder why I'm a cynic. We've got an awfully long way to go to have even a chance of getting out.'

'I'm sorry. I didn't mean to bring back those memories.' Melissa held his hand, and Chalky was still. 'Lofty, may I finish your cigarette, please?'

Chalky spoke again, embarrassed. 'Have a whole one.'

'No, no. There aren't enough. We're all in this together. I'll suffer as much as the next man. You've already saved my life once. Let's get some sleep. I have a feeling that we're going to need as much rest as we can get.'

10

We made the journey to the District Commissioner's house in silence. Gillespie had already recovered enough to be able to walk to the lorry and thence, on our arrival, into the yard to eat unaided. We were glad to be fed, and it seemed as if the entire stocks of the Commissioner's kitchens had been donated to give us one, final supper. Again we were all quiet, it was as if there was a tacit appreciation of our position, and that those around the table, so to speak, were all looking at their companions, wondering who would be next. We had all lost friends and acquaintances in our travels thus far, and knew that these travels were far from over. Though it seemed a simple task, to drive the two hundred or so miles to Myitkyina, and from there catch the first available plane, I and many others had been in this situation a number of times already. We knew we were by no means guaranteed of reaching Myitkyina, let alone catching a plane as if it were the number nine bus once we arrived. If we arrived.

The convoy left shortly after one in the afternoon. I was reminded of our journey from Yenangyaung and wondered what had become of my home. It seemed so long ago I couldn't even decide exactly how long it had been since we had left. Again we were in the midst of a long convoy of cars, and again Gillespie and myself languished in a lorry, surrounded by foodstuffs and medical supplies and some of the more useless personal possessions which we knew would be shortly thrown out. I imagined the natives finding these cases full of fine dinner suits and evening dresses and ballgowns and socks. I wondered what they would make of them. We amused ourselves by telling each other stories. Hannah told us about her mother, and her

137

wounds, and her journalist, and her sister. Gillespie and I tried to hide the feeling we had that they were all dead. She had waited long enough, and her mother had never come for her. Hannah's eyes misted up when she talked about this. Not because, as one might expect, she thought her mother was dead, but that she felt ashamed at abandoning her, at not waiting for her, for not trusting her. She seemed to feel guilty, responsible for anything which might happen, simply because she wasn't there.

We slept. It was the first time I had slept for some days; on the Assam I was always needed, especially after Gillespie's collapse. I was woken when we reached the Taping bridge. Apparently it was in a less than perfect state of repair, and there was some debate as to whether it would take the weight of a car at all. In the end we all walked across, carrying whatever supplies we felt were necessary, and then the convoy was brought across slowly, car by car, and then, with even more trepidation, lorry by lorry. In this manner, we managed to spend five hours almost stationary, in the open, and perfectly arranged for an air attack. It never came.

The road after the bridge was good, and it wasn't long before we arrived at the Kaukkwe Hills. The pass was sometimes three thousand feet up, with a sheer drop on one side, and quite exciting. The scenery was beautiful, and I spent some time showing Hannah the hills in the distance that were China. It seemed incredible that such beauty could only be fully appreciated while in such danger. I had spent fifteen or so years in Burma, and though I loved the country, it was only now, as I left, never knowing whether I would see it again, that I appreciated quite how marvellous it was. I also felt twinges of guilt that all I had done in my time here was turn a perfectly innocent plain into a smoke-belching, burning oilfield. The Burmese, of course, had been extracting oil from the Yenangyaung and Chauk plains for what must have been centuries, but we introduced new methods. Where they had dug their wells by hand, lowering a man down on a rope for what could often amount to no more than fifteen seconds work - any longer and he would be asphyxiated - we brought in derricks and nodding donkeys. It was far less dangerous than the Burmese way, but also far less romantic. As we slogged up the steep gradients, regularly abandoning cars whose engines simply were not powerful enough to pull themselves up the hill, or attempting to tow them with the far more powerful trucks, which we drove to the top, emptied, and then returned to assist the weaker vehicles, I experienced a deep sense of loss at leaving this country which had been my home for well over half my adult life. It was a sad day.

As we were far behind the schedule that someone, in his no doubt infinite wisdom, had chosen to impose on the evacuation, the decision was made, doubtless by the same humanitarian, to continue through the night. The trucks were now bringing up the rear, as the road was becoming less and less reliable. It had been built, and not very well, over marshy ground, and I imagined that come monsoon it would not be a case of trying to keep to the road, as trying to find it. Progress was painfully slow. Each bridge we came across was small, and invariably too small to cross comfortably. The beams would sag dangerously as the last trucks made their way gingerly across and more than once gave way. We lost several vehicles in this way, and also saw more than one car on its back in the river bed as we, in the group of lorries bringing up the rear, crossed. Cars became bogged down, and the trucks sank to their axles as they tried to extricate them. The potholes claimed more than one axle and by the middle of the next day, the convoy had been reduced by almost half - we left the shattered remains of over thirty vehicles in our wake. The once comfortable and spacious convoy was becoming more and more cramped as we packed ourselves into the few vehicles which remained. As we had predicted, the road behind us was not just littered with the husks of abandoned vehicles, but also with cases and trunks and bags as they had to make way for the human cargo which was felt to be more important than any mere possessions.

After three days of torturously slow progress, we came, once more, to the banks of the Irrawaddy. We were now only twenty miles or so from Myitkyina. The end was in sight. The road, however, had an entirely different idea, and here most of the remaining cars were abandoned and set on fire; the crossing was simply impassable for most of them. In the mad scramble for places within the few remaining trucks, we were left behind. We could walk, unlike many of the men travelling, and our truck had joined the long list of casualties some twenty miles before. We arrived at the river in a car, which was then destroyed, almost beneath us. Gillespie, Hannah and myself stood on the riverbank and watched as the trucks left one by one. We knew that there would be more coming, as the convoy had become somewhat spread out by this time, so we decided to wait, in order to catch a lift with one of the stragglers.

It was very late in the afternoon, and the sun was already starting to cool. Gillespie and I busied ourselves with rummaging through the possessions which had been left at the crossing, while Hannah built a fire. We had decided that, while we were waiting, we should at least find some food and, if possible, some tea. We were not disappointed, and within the hour we had sat down to a veritable feast, scavenged from the deepest recesses of abandoned luggage. We even found a bottle of whisky, which, for Gillespie and myself at least, made up for the lack of milk. We had also found a silver tea service which had been abandoned, and so sat by the side of the road drinking tea from army mugs, poured from a beautiful Georgian tea-pot. We were almost civilised. Hannah improvised a table-cloth from a wedding-dress which we found, and we must have looked a pretty picture as we sat eating with silver cutlery from a lace table-cloth, clutching our mugs of tea and with linen serviettes tucked into our filthy clothes. After we had eaten we slept for an hour, and then, realising that we were most unlikely to be picked up by a passing lorry, made the decision to walk.

A second rummage through the abandoned luggage produced two pillow-cases, which we filled with as much food and water, which we had already boiled up on our fire in preparation, as we could carry. We also picked up a walking stick each, which helped to keep our spirits up. We set off before dark.

11

The next morning the walk started with a vengeance. The sun beat down upon the refugees as they trudged for mile after mile along the railway tracks, the previous night's elation having disappeared like the morning mist, burned off by the sun and the walkers' gradual realisation of the task ahead. Lofty had a floppy hat which he gave to Melissa, in order to stop her from getting sunstroke. The two soldiers had lived outdoors for long enough to know that they were in far less danger than her. Melissa may have been bred from hardy stock, but she was still a woman, and unused to such privations. They fell further and further back along the line.

Every so often, the line would come to a stream, whereupon everybody would try to bathe, and many drank the water. Chalky made sure that they boiled it first, as after the experiences of Bustie and Jock, he simply didn't trust it. At one stream, Melissa was berating him, asking how he could possibly think the crystal clear water which fairly cascaded before them was unsafe to drink when, before he had a chance to explain, the swollen and bloated corpse of a Burmese native drifted gently by. They still bathed, taking care not to swallow the water, and let their clothes dry on them in the sun. The boy proved useful, as he was particularly suited for squeezing in and out of small gaps in the foliage when collecting kindling that no-one else could reach.

After two days, food was getting scarce, and most of the travellers would kill and eat anything they could catch. Melissa had never eaten snake before, but found her growing hunger over-rode her feeling of disgust and the bitter-sweet taste. Then, late on the third day, the column came across a train. It had been derailed through a head-on collision with another. It was full of property, and was obviously the accumulated wealth of a group of people with some power who had decided to attempt to escape with it intact. The train into which it had crashed was empty. They presumed that it was heading South to pick up more refugees. The feeling of disappointment rippled through the gathering crowd; without the greed of these people, the train would have found them, and they would be able to stop walking. Then, without warning, the crowd descended upon the carriages with the intensity of a locust swarm.

'Right. Come on Lofty. Time for you and me to throw our weight around. Food and cigarettes, that's all we want. Ready?'

'Oh yes.'

'Let's go, then.' The two men launched themselves into the throng, which by now was a heaving mass of kicking and biting people. Some were even waving their dahs about, threatening dire consequences if anyone interfered with their looting. The two Englishmen stood head and shoulders above the majority, however, and had little difficulty in finding what they were after, the rest of the refugees were still pre-occupied with loot and were also taking alcohol and clothes and money. After half an hour, they returned, to find Melissa had vanished.

'Oh god, where's she gone to now?' Chalky was distraught.

'Don't worry, I'm fine. I just did a little collecting of my own.' Melissa came back clutching a pillow-case stuffed full of foodstuffs. 'I'm going to have to spend most of the night cooking, I'm afraid. I'll need plenty of wood and water.' Chalky looked into the bag with amazement.

'Horlicks? What on earth are you going to do with Horlicks?'

'Never you mind. It looks like we'll be settling here for the night. Pick us out a spot and we'll get to work.' Chalky looked about him and realised that she was right. All about the train, men were already drinking their spoils and night fell.

'We'd better get out of this throng, with all this drink there'll be trouble tonight, that's for certain.' He looked about him. 'Lofty, what do you reckon to going on ahead for a hundred yards or so, get out of this crush?' Lofty nodded, took Melissa's bag which he slung over his shoulder and off they went.

When they had walked away from the main horde, Chalky and Lofty and the boy set about collecting water and kindling, while Melissa went to work. Within an hour they were feasting on chapattis and some fruit that the men had collected. Melissa got out the Horlicks.

'This I've got to see.' Joked Chalky, and sat smoking a

143

looted cigarette while the woman, with the help of some sugar Lofty had found, turned the chocolate powder into a passable imitation of toffee. When it had set, she wrapped it in one of the pillow cases and, using the handle of his bayonet, broke it into small pieces. She then handed them out to the astonished trio, who devoured the still-warm toffee with gusto.

'I'd be careful not to chew too hard. You might break a tooth.' She watched the men's faces light up as they sucked on the small and flaky pieces. 'Any good?'

'This, Melissa, is the most wonderful toffee I've ever eaten. When I tell my grandchildren this story they'll never believe that I had such an easy time of it.' He laughed.

'Show's not over yet.' Melissa smiled, and produced a bottle of whisky. 'Fancy a wee dram, my boys?' The smiles told her all she needed to know.

Chalky had been right about that evening. There were several fights, and he was glad he chose to set up camp away from the main horde. The next morning there were a lot of very slow walkers, and for some people the previous night's excesses had accelerated their contraction of dysentery, presumably from the amount of water they drank in the middle of the night as their bodies dehydrated. There was also a rumour that some members of the convoy had typhoid. The day was as hot, if not hotter, than before, and shoes were beginning to wear out. The column staggered along, tired, thirsty and hung-over, ill and with bleeding feet, as best it could. As Chalky and his companions were now near the head of the column, they were spared the sight of the increasing numbers of people who simply fell by the wayside, exhausted, most of them never to get up again. They also missed seeing the belongings looted from the train as they were discarded by people too tired to carry anything not entirely necessary. After another night out in the open, they finally reached Myitkyina, just before noon on the fifth day of their trek.

'Right. This is where it gets serious.' Chalky looked out across the airfield where he, and the thirteen hundred or so people left, hoped to be flown to freedom and safety. 'Jesus.' Along the runways were lines and lines of stretchers, all containing soldiers who were also waiting for a plane. 'I think we have to take the bull by the horns. Lofty, I reckon our only chance is to help people onboard. Then we may just be lucky enough to get on, too. Come on, Melissa, we'll get you out of here, see if we don't.' Melissa looked at the sunken cheeks of this man who had saved her, and realised immediately that this was the last thing he expected to be able to do. She laid her hand on his shoulder.

'Thanks for everything. I'll never forget what you've done for me.'

'Just pray to god you get the chance to. Come on.' They strode purposefully to the middle of the airfield, leaving the arriving horde of refugees stranded at the sides, still unsure what they should do. They walked past the armed guards that had been posted on the runway's perimeter. 'My wife and son.' Chalky shouted at any British soldier who lifted his rifle at them. 'I just want to see them safe.'

He reported for duty, and almost at once, the distant drone of a plane coming in to land started to fill the air. He looked at the officer to whom he was reporting, and took both the bottle of whisky and the tin of Woodbines out of his knapsack. He then presented the officer with them, and, after receiving a nod, walked directly to the point where the plane would be loaded.

'Corporal White, reporting for duty.' He shouted at the

Sergeant who looked to be in charge. He lowered his voice. 'My wife and son, Sarge.'

'Get on board, and help the wounded up when you're there. I don't expect you'll make it off the plane before it takes off, do you, Corporal?'

'No Sergeant, thank you Sergeant.' As they walked off, he turned to Melissa. 'There you are,' he whispered, 'as long as you can live with everyone thinking you're my wife, we're safe.'

'Thank you. I'm already spoken for. But I won't tell anyone if you won't.'

The plane landed, and Chalky and Lofty jumped on board, pulling the woman and the small boy on with them. 'What's my son's name, anyway?' he asked, and Melissa shrugged. 'Donald, I think. A fine name. After his grandfather.' Chalky sent them to the front of the plane while they started to load the wounded on. By this time the refugees were starting to close in and he could hear a young girl shouting at the top of her voice, but he ignored it. He knew he couldn't afford chivalry now. Soon, the plane was full, three officers climbed aboard, including the one who Chalky had "donated" his whisky and cigarettes to.

'Cigarette, Corporal?'

'Thank you, sir.' Said Chalky, as he took one of the Woodbines from the tin, and the plane taxied down the runway. 'Looks like we're out of it, sir.' He grabbed hold of one of the straps dangling from the ceiling and was suddenly reminded of London.

'Certainly does, Corporal, certainly does.' He smiled. 'Your wife, does she smoke?' The plane lifted into the air.

'Yes, sir. May I?' He reached for the tin as it was proffered to him once more, and took another cigarette. He turned to

Melissa, gave her the cigarette and was about to light it when the aircraft shuddered.

'Jesus Christ, what's happening?' The thin skin of the plane was suddenly ripped open, peppered with holes as the rushing wind and the daylight streamed in, following the path blazed by the bullets; they were back in the train. Chalky threw Melissa to the ground and lay on top of her.

'Don't worry. We'll be fine.'

12

Our final arrival in Myitkyina was in the nick of time. Gillespie was, by then, sufficiently recovered from his collapse on the Assam to attempt to walk the final twenty five miles from the river but the strain had eventually proved too much for him. He had to be hospitalised as soon as we arrived. I am sure that, had he not finally collapsed only four miles from the town, and almost within sight of it, Jeffreys and I would not have had the strength to carry him. Hannah, of course, was her usual ebullient self. After the first few days of our journey she had taken on the part of court jester, cheering us up at every available turn. I still think that she began to feel responsible for Gillespie and myself when she realised exactly how poor we were at the basics of life, like cooking. She had carried more than her fair share of luggage, all wrapped up in two pillow cases and held up on the end of the two walking sticks which we had acquired along the way.

The sight which greeted us at the hospital was quite frightening, there were hundreds of sick and wounded men lying in the hallways propped up against the walls, on trestles

and stretchers and slumped on chairs; there was no hope of
them actually being treated, that was for certain. I had noticed
that on the Assam very few attempts had been made to minister
to the wounded; one orderly wandered around injecting
morphine into the patients who made the most noise, and when
the morphine ran out, he used distilled water. Hannah elected
to stay with Gillespie while I decided to try to locate an old
friend of mine, Richard Morris, a surgical registrar who worked
at the hospital. Though a civilian, I imagined he would still be
here. It took me three hours. The hospital was labyrinthine,
packed with tiny corridors leading onto hallways which fed into
stairwells which opened out into large wards which, in their
turn, fanned out into other sets of stairwells leading to hallways
with tiny corridors disappearing off them in every direction.
The building resembled the vascular system of the human body,
the evacuated contents of which I often saw gathered in pools
in corners, waiting for a cleaner who never came. It seemed
that as soon as I was sent in one direction with information
that Richard was stationary there, he was being sucked in the
opposite direction by one of the many currents of humanity
which swirled around constantly, never allowing one to stop, to
settle, to rest. Rest in a hospital means only one thing.

I finally caught up with him as he apparently hid in a small
closet, trying to snatch a few moment's peace before he
launched himself into the river of human suffering once more.
I explained to him our situation and he suggested that I take
Gillespie to the runway. He seemed to think there was little
point in leaving him in the hospital. He was so tired and fraught
he seemed to be on the verge of giving up all of his patients for
dead. I had never seen a man changed so much, from the once
jolly and avuncular doctor who made his rounds with pockets

bursting with sweets and his patter bursting with little jokes, to this pale and wasted specimen I saw in front of me. He knew that if we took Gillespie to the plane someone else would be left behind, but, as he explained, someone was going to be left behind, and if he could possibly prevent that from being anyone he knew, he would. I had the feeling that he was unwilling to allow anyone who knew him witness what he plainly believed to be his final descent. He signed some papers for me and told me to present them to the Sergeant on duty on the runway, and that there was a plane due within the hour. I thanked him as best I could and made my way slowly back to where I had left Hannah and Gillespie. I had been gone for almost four hours. No-one had even looked at him. Hannah was downcast as I approached, but as I explained the chit I had, she became excited once more, and we eased Gillespie into a wheelchair that I managed to appropriate, and made for the airfield.

It took us half an hour to negotiate the checkpoints and gates, and when we finally arrived, we were greeted with a scene of absolute devastation. All one could see, in any direction, were thousands of refugees all sitting quietly and still in the blistering heat, with no water and no food, no shelter, and hundreds of stretchers and wounded men lined up along the runway's edge. It was truly horrific. I knew immediately we had no chance of getting Gillespie on the next plane, there were simply too many people waiting. We decided to have a go anyway. Hannah's face was not one which invited disappointment; she expected us to succeed, so I thought that maybe we would.

There was a system of perimeters in operation, whereby each of the enclosures contained men whose evacuation was deemed more imperative than the men in the previous perimeter. We had negotiated two of them, our progress hampered by our lack of suitable material for bribes, when we heard the plane approaching. As one, the entire mass of refugees and soldiers became silent, and those sitting rose to their feet, and everyone stared into the sky, searching for the saviour that they must have known would never be able to provide them succour. As it neared the field, and eventually, wheels screeching, landed, the mass seemed to walk a few steps closer like a cricketer, walking in towards the batsman as the ball is bowled. We were too far away to stand a chance of gaining passage, and I was about to turn the wheelchair around in search of a better plan, when Hannah suddenly shrieked and started to run towards the plane, which, having landed, was now being loaded and refuelled with what appeared to be almost indecent haste.

I stopped in my tracks, and then, after laying my hand on the helpless Gillespie's shoulder, I gave chase. She squeezed past the first row of guards easily enough, with far more ease than I managed; I had to beg and plead, explain that she was my daughter, until they let me past. As we neared the aircraft, the crowd became thicker as it seemed everyone within range had decided to simply rush the plane in the vain hope that the fates would smile on them and let them climb on board. I heard gunshots. What Hannah was so excited about, I had no idea. I fought and pushed and kicked like everybody else to get close to the plane, but in my case it was to remove someone, not to gain entry.

When I had got to within fifty feet or so of the plane, I saw the doors slide shut, and the crowd pulled back momentarily as the engines started up, propellers arcing lazily in the air before the real power kicked in and they turned into a spinning haze of black. The plane started to inch forward and I saw Hannah standing alone, twenty feet from the plane, shouting herself hoarse, tears streaming down her cheeks. I rushed up to grab her just as she was about to give chase, and the plane pulled away down the runway. I held her face up to mine and asked her what on earth had got into her. I was angry. She simply looked at me, dumbfounded and then quietly, almost apologetically, she said "My mother. My mother is on that plane." I hugged her and looked up as the plane took off rather shakily and the crowd started to dissipate. I turned around and, with the distraught Hannah clasped to my chest, I walked slowly back to were I had left the hapless Gillespie. It was then we heard the noise that we all dreaded; the Japanese air force.

The plane which had just taken off, full of refugees and wounded, was attacked first, when it had barely put three hundred feet of air between itself and the ground it so desperately wanted to flee. The fighters chased and harried it like a pack of dogs after a wounded deer and, as was inevitable, it crashed, skidding back across the runway and into the fields beyond. The fighters kept on strafing it as the runway cleared of refugees, we all ran, screaming, as fast as we could away from the scene. There was no thought but away.

The fighters, however, were not content with the plane. Having become bored with their initial prey, they left it bloodied and burning as they turned their attention to the strafing of the long lines of wounded that were still laid out on the runway's edge. It was like something out of a funfair. It was impossible to see how much more could have been done to present the Japanese with an easier target. They wheeled and fired for what seemed like hours, and Hannah and I lay in the thick shrub surrounding the runway, Hannah with her hands over her ears crying. We had left Gillespie behind. He had been on the end of one of the long lines.

13

It was probably the most difficult thing I have ever had to do; dragging the silent yet tearful Hannah away from the smouldering wreck of a plane which contained the remains of her mother. I, for one, was unsure that she really had been on board, as in such times of stress it is easy to see what one wants to see, even what one expects to see. After the privations she had endured since leaving Rangoon it was not surprising that she assumed the worst. I certainly hoped that it wasn't her mother who she had seen, merely someone who looked similar, wore some clothes which she recognised, but whenever I broached the subject, I was stared down; Hannah wouldn't say one word. It was as if we were back in Pagan, with her sitting silently in the car waiting for something to happen, except that this time the only thing she could be waiting for was death.

Having lost Gillespie during the raid, and having mislaid Jeffreys during the march when he managed to scramble onto a truck, we were alone. The scenes at the airfield were calamitous. It seemed that the raid had increased everyone's desire to escape now, and somehow fuelled their desperation to travel by air. The seething mass of refugees was choking the runway so that, even if there was to be another plane, which I doubted now, it would never be able to land. One thing I did know was that there was nowhere to walk to from Myitkyina. If we were to escape, we were going to have to go by foot, and the only options from Myitkyina were China or an attempt to reach Assam through the Kumon hills. Neither of these appealed, and the general consensus amongst the few officers I met was that there were two available routes, one through the Hawkaung valley, the other via Homalin and the Upper Chindwin to Dimapur, a similar route to the one I should have taken some time before. I decided that we should simply see where we ended up, as each route involved us returning into the heart of Burma, and thus closer to the Japanese. So far, any concrete decision I had made regarding my escape had proved fruitless, so I resisted the temptation to formulate a new plan. At the station we found a train sitting there, calmly waiting to return to Mogaung. Here both routes were available. We boarded it.

It was a hospital train that had only recently arrived. It was also crowded to the extent that the compartment in which we found ourselves, designed to take four people in relative comfort, was crammed with six times that number. The smell was appalling, and the close proximity of our fellow passengers was in great contrast to our journey thus far. Up until now we had, if nothing else, space to breath and move, even if the air had been laden with oil fumes and wood smoke. Now we could hardly breath, and did not even want to, the air was so foul. Not only did we have to contend with the individual smells of each other, and as everyone had been on the road for some time, these were not inconsiderable, but there was still the residual odour of the train's previous incumbents, as well as being numerous stains on the seats and floor to indicate where the wounded had lain. The remaining windows in each carriage lasted for mere minutes before they were pushed out from the inside, by common consent.

We were lucky. We had managed to get a place close to a window, and Hannah sat on the edge of the seat while I stood. Underneath her feet she held the last vestiges of our supplies; yet another bottle of whisky, this time donated by the good doctor, some tins of the staple bully beef and two canteens of fresh water. All of this was wrapped in a discarded army pack

I had picked up from the road. Hannah sat with her blanket across her knees. She held tightly onto my hand as the carriage juddered and twitched like an old man trying to get out of his chair. There were so many people on board that it had trouble pulling away from the station, but finally we limped away from Myitkyina and the scenes of devastation, wondering all the while what was still in store for us.

Myitkyina to Mogaung is not a long journey, only forty miles or so. It took this patched-up, wheezing and asthmatic old train nine hours to cover the distance. Several times, when the combination of gradient and over-loading was simply too much for it to bear, it ground to a halt. The first time we simply stopped, and then some officers walked up and down the side of the train calling on people to get out and push. I climbed out of the window, leaving Hannah behind with a revolver and strict instructions not to let anyone push her out of her seat or steal our supplies, followed by a number of others. There were not enough, and the two officers took to waving their pistols about until the rest of the able-bodied passengers exited and began to push the train up the hill. It was a strange sight, and when we reached the top there was an almighty scramble to try to claim seats not previously occupied. It seemed that in times of stress, even the most basic of manners are forgotten. I found the window by far the easiest entrance, and spent much of the journey hanging out of it.

Our arrival at Mogaung was met with surprise. It seemed that the few officials there were expecting mere hundreds of refugees, and that they had felt that they could deal with these numbers. Unaware of the fate which had befallen Myitkyina, they were unprepared for the thousands of people who now swamped them from both directions. Their plans were plainly a little inadequate. I made myself available to the planning officers and it was decided, after much argument and deliberation, to try the route through the Hawkaung valley; it was felt that any trek through the Upper Chindwin would be difficult to supply en route, especially considering the numbers now involved. It was also felt that the Chindwin route held a greater risk of meeting the Japanese and the few of us who were capable of bearing what little armaments we had were certainly in no condition to deal with that, much less possessed of a desire to. We managed to requisition five lorries to take us the first few miles, agreeing that we should return three of them to pick up more refugees after the first day, and keep two to ferry the worst of the wounded as far as we could along the road, which was little more than a bullock track. We organised ourselves quickly and set off early the next morning, as the rains were not far away and as soon as they came the only way we would be able to move would be on foot. While we had transport, we were determined to make the best of it.

We packed merely the bare essentials, crowded ourselves into the lorries and left Mogaung. It was a grey and misty morning, and there had already been a little rain, though not enough to hamper our progress. As we pulled out we all tried to avoid looking back; all we saw when we did so was the crowd of refugees not fortunate enough to join our party looking with eyes of disappointment and fear. I did not envy them their trek. They would have to walk the entire way. The atmosphere inside the lorries was dark and sombre. We all knew we were lucky, if you could call driving into the jungle at the beginning of the monsoon in order to, eventually, walk what would be over two hundred miles through thick jungle and narrow hill passes lucky.

In the first day we managed over fifty miles. We made camp by the side of the road and organised ourselves for the next day, during which we would only have the use of two lorries. The mood in the camp was still dark, and there was not much conversation as each group made a meagre supper of bully beef and tea. We were now deep in Kachin territory, and in order to keep ourselves alive, we knew we would soon have to barter with the villagers for food. May of them, however, seemed to have disappeared, presumably scared off by this sudden influx of foreigners through their lands. The next morning we set off once more, this time using the lorries as ferries, driving them backwards and forwards, shuttling the group onwards, and our progress slowed accordingly. The track was starting to become more difficult, as well, and each lorry was now accompanied by men who would continually cut great swathes of plant matter from the jungle to lay on the track in order to allow the lorries to gain traction over the most muddy parts. When we came across mud which was too deep, we would simply cut a new path through the jungle. It was a little like the early days of the century, when each vehicle was preceded by a man with a red flag. We came across several other vehicles abandoned along the way, and managed to extricate and mend some of them, making us more mobile.

If we were disappointed at only making half the distance on the second day that we had managed on the first, the third saw us having to abandon most of our newly-acquired vehicles to the mud, and we finally reached Lakyens, some hundred miles from Mogaung, as dusk was falling on the third day. Now we knew that there was no way forward other than on foot.

14

We walked into Lakyens tired, wet and cold. The rations we had brought with us were beginning to run out and several of the party were suffering from dysentery, myself included. Hannah had, since the airfield incident, turned from the happy, bright young girl who had come out of her shell that first night after we found her, into a sullen, miserable child. It was, however, as if she were the touchstone for the group, reflecting the feelings the rest of us had but refused to show. Our stubbornness was never more apparent than now; we simply refused to think about the privations we were suffering, not only because we knew others were in a far worse state than us, but we also knew that conditions were likely to deteriorate still further. Hannah not only refused to speak, ignoring our feeble attempts to keep up our morale through increasingly banal conversation, but also refused to give up the blanket she had adopted earlier, clutching onto it as she walked alongside me even as it became wet and presumably heavy, as if it were her only contact with a better time. Lakyens was where the party split up into smaller groups; it was obvious that we could not continue our trek together.

We were the last to leave, as I was struck down with malaria, and spent three unpleasant days confined to a bed of rush matting while Hannah watched over me, all the while saying nothing. She simply sat and stared, sentinel-like, still clutching her blanket. The only human contact I had was the occasional visit from a doctor who was with the party, though he left on the second day, leaving me with some medicine, and a missionary who arrived soon after him. He made me drink a native rice wine that was extremely potent, and apparently a traditional native cure, and talked about his journey so far. He was travelling with his wife and an elephant. Sometimes it seemed to me that I was hallucinating, making up the memories I have of him as I never did see it, but it was there, apparently; Hannah later told me that she saw it, was introduced to it even, and that it was called Mary. There were moments when I felt I would never get out of that bed.

Luckily, I recovered sufficiently to begin the walk, though whether it was the missionary's medicine or not I don't know, and we finally left with the last group, having gathered together as much food and equipment as we could carry. There had been some bullock carts bought to transport rations by the other groups but, by the time we were ready to leave, there were none left. It was a sorry-looking and weary bunch of twelve walking wounded and one miserable and silent girl who left Lakyens that day.

Our first stop was the Taphai Kha crossing at Taipha. The river was flowing fast, too fast for one man who tried to swim and was swept away by the current as we all watched, open-mouthed in horror. The raft could only take twenty people at a time and when we arrived it was sinking under the weight of over thirty men who were struggling and fighting to get across. There was a tangible air of panic, but soon order was restored and within a few hours the crowd was dispersed. We were all tired and managed to buy some food at the village, chicken and rice which was stuffed into hollowed-out tubes of bamboo and boiled. In the afternoon we only managed to get as far as the next crossing, at N'Kyaw, where we decided to stay for the night. It was here that the first storm hit us as we tried to sleep in the bamboo hut, which like the rest of the village was built on stilts, which we had hired. It was anything but waterproof, and the rush mats which passed for windows proved to be no barrier to the wind which blew torrents of water through them, soaking us all and chilling us to the bone. The storm lasted until the next afternoon when we left, even more weary and bedraggled than we had been on arrival. At least we had eaten well, and the memory of this food kept us going through the next day. The storm had rendered the path very muddy and slippery, and had blown over many trees, so passage was even more difficult than before. Hannah walked beside me, one hand clutching the tails of my shirt while the other held her beloved blanket close to her face. The entire group walked in silence.

It was not only for us that the path was becoming difficult. It was very narrow, and many of the trekkers who had gone before us had managed to buy ponies to carry their rations, and we seemed to pass another carcass every mile. It had not got to the stage, though it could not be far away, that the death of a pony was a cause for rejoicing, as it meant a welcome addition to rations.

Our next target was the village of Shimbyiyang, where we were expecting to receive new rations. There was a rumour, though how these things start in the middle of the jungle is beyond me, that this village was being targeted by allied planes which were dropping food and other supplies. This idea kept us going through the four days during which we struggled through the jungle, wet, tired and weak.

Every night since we had left N'Kyaw, we camped in the open, cutting a hole in the jungle by the side of the path, the thirteen of us sleeping as close to one another as we possibly could. Hannah would wrap herself in her blanket, after trying to dry it on a fire, if we had managed to make one, and I would let her sleep using me as a wind-break, encircling her in my arms and holding her as close as I could. It had been over a week since she had said a word. As she had done at Pagan, she refused to let me out of her sight, forcing me, much to my embarrassment, to accompany her when she needed to go to the toilet, even following me when I went. We managed to eat at another village, but refused to stay as we knew that Shimbyiyang was only another fifteen miles distant. It seemed imperative to all of us to reach it that day, as morale was sinking very low, so we forged on ahead, ignoring tired limbs and the failing light. The final three hours of that day were walked in total darkness. We were silent, following the sound of feet as they fell into the mud immediately in front of us. Occasionally a fallen tree would break the quiet as we heard the pain of the leading man as he walked directly into it. The only light was from the fireflies which seemed to dart around us like fairies, and we were plagued by mosquitoes.

We had all but given up hope when the bark of a dog up ahead signalled that the end of this particular journey was drawing near, and we managed to drag ourselves into the village, where we dried ourselves before fires and slept, the night being dry for the first time in what seemed like weeks, but was only three days. Not one of us dared mention that our journey had only just begun.

The next morning we were woken by the sound of planes. The first thought we had was shared; the Japanese. Luckily, we were wrong, and on leaving our hut, we saw a lone plane dropping parachutes, not far from the village. We ran to see what they had given us. It truly was manna from heaven. When we arrived where we reckoned the parachutes had fallen, we were greeted by the sight of a clearing, within which there were three of the fallen packages, their wings gently billowing in the breeze. We rushed to them and found that each one was a bag of rice. This as a little disappointing, until one of our number discovered a fourth package which had fallen into the jungle and burst. The rice was primarily padding. Buried inside the bags were tins of bully beef, condensed milk, medicine, tea, sugar, biscuits and, wonder of wonders, tins of cigarettes. We were not the only men at the village so the rations were divided up, allowing each man enough for six days. This was how long we were expected to take to reach the next camp which had supplies.

With food and cigarettes, and after a night that wasn't cold and wet, the group's morale soared. We were warm and dry, and we had tea and cigarettes. In the afternoon we set off once more, but this time without the heavy hearts which had hampered us over the last leg. I half-expected that Hannah would break her vow of silence, but I was disappointed.

15

It took us ten days to traverse the next section of our journey. The going was very difficult, the mud from the rains slowed us almost as much as the increasingly hilly country tired us. We were plagued by leeches, which seemed to be able to crawl into the most tightly secured of places, and which, after a day's march, would have to be carefully removed with the blade of a knife or a burning cigarette. The temptation to merely rip or brush them off had to be resisted as this invariably led to an infected wound, and many of the party were by now suffering from dysentery, despite our careful boiling of the water, to add to the wounds that they already carried.

The pathway was by now becoming almost choked with refugees, and each night we made camp as best we could, erecting makeshift huts of bamboo and leaves which merely slowed down the rate at which we became soaked. It was raining almost every night now, and it became increasingly difficult to make fires with which to cook our fast diminishing stores of food. At one point we stumbled across a slow-moving party of over a hundred men, many of whom were native porters. It was the Governor of Burma making his escape. He travelled with his wife, dogs and even a pet ape, which apparently clung bad-tempered to the back of a bodyguard the entire way. We managed to beg some provisions from them, mainly saccharine which was a very useful supplement to our diet, making our tea far more palatable and warming, on the few occasions when we managed a good brew-up. Of the ten days travel, only two were dry, and on these we made up a lot of ground, leaving the slow-moving governor's party behind.

As the trail lengthened, the parties which travelled together became smaller and smaller, and ours became enmeshed with about sixty natives with whom we tended to make camp. Most of the clearings which we used seemed as if they had been occupied the previous night, festooned as they were with discarded milk and bully beef cans; sanitation was becoming an ever more pressing problem, and we began to pass exhausted, ill and dead men more regularly. This was distressing to all of us but we were having enough trouble keeping ourselves going, so could not afford to try to assist anybody else. The feeling of helplessness when you pass a man by the side of the path who is lying, exhausted, and plainly close to death is not an experience I would care to repeat.

The rivers we now met were swollen by the rains, and more than once we struggled to find a point which was shallow enough for us to wade through. We lost one member of our party during such a crossing, as he was hit by a stray branch in the river and lost his footing, as well as three others for whom the combination of their wounds, their lack of food and their dysentery became too much. It was with heavy hearts that we left them, hoping against hope that they would recover enough strength in a day or two to join up with another group.

We finally reached our ultimate destination, the Paungsa Pass and India. It took us some hours to make the final journey, as we had by now run out of food and were all seriously weakened. The pass barely qualified as a path and was extremely steep and muddy, and on more than one occasion we travelled without the aid of our legs, sliding dangerously down the slope. At the bottom, however, we arrived at what to us was a veritable heaven. The Indian Tea Planter's Association had set up camps in India to receive the refugees coming out of the jungle, and this was the first. We ate heartily and slept.

From here we set off after one day's rest, though the fact that we had, effectively, finished our trials energised us. No-one would consider giving up now, no matter how tired or ill they felt. The path, however, had other ideas, and a combination of the monsoon's steadily increasing grip on the country and the fact that there was now two-way traffic, we passed many coolies and mules heading for the camp with food, made this part of the journey the most difficult yet. We trudged it with happy hearts, however, moving from camp to camp, eating progressively more each day, our shrunken stomachs suffering the consequences. At times the mud was knee-deep, and ropes had been set up so the bogged-down could extricate themselves. Thus we walked from Burma to the camps at Nampong, Namchick and Kumlao.

We finally arrived at Margharita, where a collection point was being organised for refugees, before the main gathering-point at Ledo, after almost three weeks of travel. It was here that we realised exactly how we must have looked. Our clothes were tattered and torn, few of us had boots which were worthy of the name, and we were all heavily bearded. We were given new clothes, razors and water and within an hour the eight of us who remained, as well as Hannah, sat down to a meal clean and dry for the first time in weeks. Hannah was still silent, and still clutched at her blanket, though she had consented for it to be cleaned. We spent a moment in silence, thinking of those we knew who had failed to get this far before eating as if we were never to receive another meal. I for one spent most of the night regretting this indulgence.

The next day we all parted. I, along with four others, elected to stay in order to assist the refugees who would soon be flooding the camp, while three others were to return to the remains of their regiments. Hannah and I watched as they climbed into the back of a lorry and were driven away. Two of the remaining men were already in hospital, and I imagined that this was where most of us would be before long, as the final escape deprived our bodies of the need to carry on. Before I reported for duty, I talked to one of the officers in charge of the camp and discovered that there was a plane leaving later that day, and I arranged for Hannah to take it.

We sat by the edge of the airfield, sheltering from the rain under a tarpaulin, as an open cock-pitted plane wheeled in to land. The pilot rushed out and, after some consultation with the duty officer, was pointed in our direction. He made a dash from his tarpaulin to ours.

'Pras Tata.' He said, extending his right hand. I took it and shook it vigorously. 'Barnes says that this is your daughter.' He ruffled Hannah's hair playfully and she giggled. It was the first smile I had seen from her since Myitkyina. Through his flying helmet he looked to be a very dark native, but he removed it to reveal the light skin of a Parsee. 'I hate the monsoon. Don't you?'

'Yes. Thank you very much for agreeing to take Hannah. I've got to stay, but she needs to get out.'

'Where should I take her?' I was confused. I had no idea where my own wife and daughter had gone, except that they had gone via Calcutta.

'Well, my wife and…' I hesitated, and Pras looked at me strangely.

'Do I know you..?' he began. I smiled nervously.

'Calcutta. Get her to the British Consulate, or the offices of Burmah Oil. Her mother is there, somewhere. Name of Painton.' I dropped down to Hannah and whispered in her ear, 'remember that name. Tell my wife that I'll be home soon. Wherever home is. And give her this.' I kissed her on both cheeks. 'And you look after Margaret for me. She's my real daughter. You'll like her.' I hugged her and Pras looked at me, then smiled and turned to walk back to the plane. Hannah looked up, a tear in her eye.

'Thank you. Goodbye.' They were her first words since Myitkyina. She reached up, kissed me and ran towards the plane, still clutching her blanket. I was wearing all that I owned. All I had arrived at the camp with was the three rolls of film I had collected at Pagan.

Two days later the strain caught up with me and I was hospitalised, suffering from a combination of exhaustion, dysentery and malaria — I had lost over four stone during the trek. I spent the next two months convalescing before I was finally able to help with the continuing influx of refugees. The Hawkaung valley was only one of many routes used to escape, and records suggest that over twenty thousand arrived at the camps in Margharita and Ledo. There are no records of how many died. The trek continued here until July, even though the camps were deemed unusable in June due to the monsoon conditions. There were still refugees in these camps in November of nineteen forty-two.

I was unable to leave until after Christmas.

about the author

sometime academic, lapsed musician and general ne'erdowell pete langman would have been a celebrated Dickensian character had he not had the good fortune to be born in a time of more expert dental care.

Made in the USA
Charleston, SC
27 January 2014